DAVID NETH

FUSE

ORIGIN

BOOK 1

 Publishing

Origin
Fuse, Book 1
Copyright © 2017 by David Neth
Batavia, NY

www.DavidNethBooks.com

Publisher: David Neth
Editing: Amy Maddox of The Blue Pencil
Proofreading: John Ognibene

ISBN: 978-1-945336-86-7
First edition

Subscribe to the author's newsletter for updates and exclusive content:
DavidNethBooks.com/Newsletter

Follow the author at:
www.facebook.com/DavidNethBooks
www.twitter.com/DavidNethBooks
www.instagram.com/dneth13

CHAPTER ONE

I was going to grab some lunch. Do you want to join?" Emma asks, stepping into my cubicle space. She pushes up her thick-rimmed glasses and smiles. Her blonde hair is pulled away from her face. She happens to be my girlfriend. When I started at Wyatt, Emma took me under her wing and showed me the ropes. We've been inseparable ever since.

I stretch out on my chair before standing. "Sounds good to me. Did you brown-bag it today or are we heading over to the mall?" The Grid—named after the layout of the streets downtown—is a mall located across the street from the Wyatt Building. It's another scar the city has from its decline.

"There's actually a new café that just opened downstairs. You want to try it?"

"Sure." I grab my wallet and hoodie and follow her to the elevator.

The Buzzing Bar is packed.

"Guess that's what we get for going to the newest place downtown at lunchtime," Emma says, motioning to the crowd.

"You're right, but this'll be fine. I read online that they have fresh-baked raisin bread here." Her favorite.

"Ooooo!" Her eyes light up as a smile spreads across her face. "I'm gonna have to get me some of that."

I laugh and wrap my arm around her as the line shuffles forward.

After we get our food, we head upstairs and sit on the windowsill by the elevators, scarfing down our sandwiches before our lunch break ends.

"Tomorrow we bring our own lunches." I ball the sandwich paper and toss it in the garbage in the corner. I miss, but I don't move to pick it up.

Emma nods and tucks a loose piece of her blonde hair behind her ear. "So Mr. Marble wants to meet with me at three today."

"What about?" Mr. Marble is the director of the Wyatt Industries corporate office. Typically the IT department answers to the IT manager, but once Henry Haney left, we've been without one for months. Word around the office is that Marble is looking to shrink the IT department to save on expenses.

Emma shrugs. "I don't know."

"Do you think he's going to cut you loose?" I ask.

She leans forward and buries her face in her hands. "Oh God, I hope not!"

I place a hand on her shoulder, regretting my words. They have a habit of slipping out accidentally. "I doubt that's it. Maybe he just wants you to spend a week at the plant. That's what happened to Craig. They promoted him and sent him off to the plant for their systems IT."

"Yeah, but I'm not even qualified for that!"

Emma's degree is in business administration. She only got the job because she worked in the IT department in college.

She closes her eyes. "I can't lose this job!"

"Emma, chill. You don't even know what he wants, right? Just go to the meeting and take it from there."

"You're right," she says with a sigh. "We should get back." She kisses me on the cheek. "Thanks, Ethan."

It's raining by the time I see Emma head up to Marble's office.

CHAPTER ONE

With the dark storm clouds blocking any natural light, my cubicle feels even more like a box. The fluorescent lights are almost blinding compared to the dark skies outside. Cracks of thunder boom every so often, growing increasingly more frequent as the storm lets loose on the city.

An hour and a half passes and Emma's still not back yet. My knee bounces up and down as I write up my report for the last call I took. I can't focus on what I'm saying, so I make an excuse to myself that I need to go to the bathroom. I wonder if the meeting was too stressful for her to talk about how it went so she went home without saying good-bye. That doesn't sound like her, though.

Her purse is tucked under her desk and her desk lamp is still on when I pass by, so I know she definitely hasn't left yet. I figure I might as well continue the trip to the bathroom, but someone stops me before I can even exit the office.

"Hey, buddy, I need some service on this piece of shit my wife calls a computer." The man's belly hangs over his pants and his sleeves are rolled up, showing off his hairy forearms. His voice booms throughout the office, and I see several heads look up over the walls of their cubicles to see who it is.

He presses the laptop against my chest, and I take it from him.

"What's the problem?"

"It's too damn slow! I need a cleanup or whatever you guys do." He's backing away from me now. He's probably used to ordering people around—especially people like me who, despite the fact that I'm twenty-five, look like they should still be in high school. "My name's John Bemurzeski. I'm on nine. I need it by tomorrow." He's out the door before I can respond.

Sighing, I head back to my desk and write a Post-it on the laptop. *John B-something, 9th floor. Needs by tomorrow.*

Before I can open it up to turn it on, I have a call coming in on my headset. I walk the lady on the phone through a software update. By the time I'm off the phone, the office has already cleared out. I look at the clock and see that it's twenty after five. I'm usually halfway home by now.

5

Fuse: Origin

The storm is growing louder. I look out the window for a minute. I know I can't go home yet. I need to work on the laptop the guy brought in. He'll probably be here first thing in the morning for it. I figure by the time I'm finally able to go home, the storm will either have passed or be at its peak. Plus, I'm still worried about Emma's meeting. At the very least, I want to walk her to the subway.

Craning my neck over the cubicle wall, I can see lightning striking down on the suburbs on the outskirts of the city. Nope. This is definitely the peak now. What a great vantage point to enjoy the storm!

My enthusiasm dies when I open the laptop. The thing is moving at a snail's pace. My frustration mounts as it takes three times as long as it should to open a web browser and connect to Wyatt's wi-fi. I pull up solitaire on my computer and play around while I wait for the laptop to load.

I think about Emma. It's well after five and she's still up with Marble. I decide to head up and see what's taking her so long when the browser on the laptop finally loads.

Low battery.

I fuss with the cord John dropped off and plug it into the computer. The power strip by my desk is all full, so I carry the laptop over to the main power line that runs through the center of the building. Nothing like taking energy right from the source. Plus, it gives me an excuse to check out the storm.

The lights flicker, and I hear a crack of thunder as I plug the computer in. My fingers slip onto one of the prongs.

In an instant I feel a jolt travel up my arm and throughout my body. The next moment, the world goes black.

CHAPTER TWO

'm exhausted. Too tired to open my eyes or even move. I try to take in as much as I can using my other senses.

I'm covered by warm blankets. A nice warm cocoon, but I feel something irritating my chest. Multiple somethings. My hand drags across my body as I try to feel for whatever it is. Something cold and plastic. I feel other strings of plastic running under a thin piece of fabric that covers my body, taped to various places on my chest. I have a tube running along my face and into my nose, but the air I'm breathing seems clear, fresh. A beep chimes with each breath.

My hand slinks back down to my side, and I hear someone's voice. I can't make out what they say, who it is, or even if it's a man or a woman.

Slowly, I open my eyes and look around. There's a lamp on the opposite wall offering soft light, but most of the room is still dark. I'm in a hospital bed, which clarifies the beeping and the various cords on me.

My right arm is wrapped in a thick layer of gauze. I can't quite move it, but I still feel a tingling running up and down it.

FUSE: ORIGIN

How did I end up here? I can't even remember what day it is. Panic sets in.

I was at work. Worried about Emma up in Marble's office and then . . .

My assessment is cut short when I hear clicking heels coming down the hall. My eyes shift—I'm still too tired to move my head—and I see Emma enter with another woman.

"Mr. Pierce," the woman starts. She's wearing a white lab coat and what looks like black scrubs underneath. She's holding a clipboard with a page flipped over the top and the end of it pressed against her stomach. "Can you hear me, Mr. Pierce?" She leans down and lays a hand on my good arm.

I search for my voice, unsure of how it will sound or if I even have the energy for it. I open my mouth, but nothing comes out at first. Eventually a croak escapes. It's not my voice, that's for sure.

The woman's skin stretches as she smiles. She pats my arm and I'm suddenly hot—embarrassed to be in such a state in front of such a classy woman.

"Are you feeling any pain?"

"Tired," I manage to say in my damaged voice. At least it's clearer this time.

She nods and smiles again. "You should get some more rest. It's been a rough few days. You need to rebuild your strength. Sleep."

I close my eyes and wonder what she meant by "few days." Surely I haven't been here that long, have I? Why am I here in the first place? What happened in that office?

———

WHEN I WAKE again, I feel much more energized. The cords on my chest are gone, and the gauze on my arm has been replaced with a smaller wrap. My fingers are still tingling, but it's not as strong as it was the last time I was awake. Whenever that was.

"Ethan." I hear a familiar voice—my brother's. Cale.

Chapter Two

I look toward the sound of his voice. It takes a moment for my eyes to focus on his face.

"How are you feeling?"

"Better," I say. I sound more like myself, but it's still not my regular voice. It's my early-morning, just-woke-up voice.

He squeezes my shoulder, and I reach up and place my hand on his.

"You scared the shit out of us, man," he says.

I finally notice Myra. She stands beside Cale and takes my hand while hooking her arm around him. Her dark complexion is flawless. Her naturally curly hair frames her face. She always smells like coconut—likely a result of the mousse that's required to tame her mass of curls.

She's Councilman Frank Lloyd's assistant, so she's always in professional attire for her job at city hall. Her heart is invested in the city and everyone she meets.

Myra squeezes my hand. "I'm so glad you're awake."

"What happened?"

Cale looks confused. "You don't remember?"

"Not really."

"You were electrocuted," Myra says. "Emma found you in your office. I guess you were plugging something in when the antenna on top of the building was struck."

Pieces of my memory begin to come back. Writing out the Post-it. Playing solitaire. Fumbling with the cord. "Oh. Yeah, that's right."

"You've been in and out of consciousness for a week now," Cale continues. "They were afraid of what kind of damage had been done. Judging from the stupid look on your face, I'm guessing brain damage." He grins.

Myra rolls her eyes and swats his arm. "Don't listen to him. Dr. Fletcher says you're doing great."

"I brought your mail." Cale hands me a small stack of envelopes. "It's been piling up on the counter, and I figured it'd give you something to do while you're here."

The stack is full of cards from relatives and coworkers. I wonder how many of them have come in to see me while I was out. The one that stands out is from Tranidek Energy. My address is handwritten so I open it first.

Mr. Ethan Pierce,

It's hard to miss the headlines detailing your accident. As someone who has worked with energy his whole life, I can attest how lucky you are. Throughout my career I've lost a number of friends in accidents similar to yours. On behalf of all of us here at Tranidek Energy, we wish you a speedy recovery.

You must be wondering why someone from a competing company to your employer is writing to you. When I read about a fellow Olympian subjected to that much electricity who lived, well, I just had to reach out to him. Upon further research, I've uncovered parts of your work experience and I'm very impressed.

Once you're well and rested, I'd love to speak to you in person about your future. To aid in your focus on recovery, I would like to offer for Tranidek Energy to pay all of your medical bills for your time in the hospital.

Your story is remarkable, and I'd love to have Tranidek be a part of it.

Frank Rizzoli
President and CEO of Tranidek Energy

My mouth hangs open when I finish reading.

"What?" Cale asks, snatching the letter from me. Myra reads over his shoulder, and I watch as their eyes grow as they read.

"Ethan, this is huge!" Myra beams.

"How the hell did they get our address?"

I shrug. "Maybe from Wyatt? I don't know. What do you think I should do?"

"What do you mean?" Cale asks incredulously. "Ethan, they're paying *all* of your medical bills. Give them anything they want!"

Chapter Two

"Yeah, but I work for their competitor. And they want to talk about my future? There's gotta be strings attached."

"Sounds like they might want to offer you a job," Myra says.

I'm not sure I want to leave Wyatt. Sure, my job isn't the most exciting, but I like it. I've been there long enough that I've grown comfortable. Plus, I get to see Emma. I'm content. Besides, would Tranidek be able to match what I'm making now?

I look up and spot my parents walking in. Mom gives me a tight hug that lasts a few minutes. When she pulls away, she wipes at her eyes. Dad squeezes my shoulder.

"Glad to see you're awake. How do you feel?" he asks.

"Tired, but otherwise okay." I hand them the letter. "I got this in the mail."

They both skim through it.

My mother, always the skeptic, says, "I don't know . . . "

"I'd talk to them first before you accept any money from them," Dad says.

"Yeah, I will." Whenever I get out of here.

"How're the doctors and everyone treating you?" Mom asks. "We have nice one out by us that you might want to transfer to. It's probably cheaper and—"

"Mom, this is the closest one to where *I* live," I say. The First Olympian Medical Center is right downtown, only a few blocks from work.

"Besides, this is the city's top-rated hospital," Myra adds.

"That one by you guys is such a joke of a hospital anyway," Cale says. "You hear horror stories all the time!"

"Well, maybe after you're released you can come stay with us for a bit," Mom insists.

"I'll be fine."

"But you're going to need help getting around."

"What about me?" Cale asks.

Mom waves a hand dismissively. "You're always working."

Dad puts his arm around her. "They'll figure it out. And we're not *that* far."

Mom lets out a deep breath but doesn't say anymore.

"Cale and I both think that you're getting the best service

11

here. Your doctor is one of the top recommended in Olympia," Myra says.

"Doesn't hurt that's she's smoking hot, either." Cale raises his eyebrows.

"Cale!" Mom shouts.

"Mr. Pierce," the woman with the white lab coat enters again. "I'm assuming by the smile on your face that you're feeling much better?"

I nod slowly, happy that I'm not as exhausted as I was before.

"Good. We want to run a few more tests, but I'm hoping to get you sitting up and maybe even eating before the day is over," she says. "Your vitals all seem to have leveled out. We'll monitor you to determine what our next steps will be for your recovery."

"How much longer do you think I'll be here?" I notice her name tag says Dr. Alex Fletcher. My brother was right. She's beautiful.

"That depends on how much effort you put into your recovery. I'm going to bring in a physical therapist tomorrow to see how well you do on your feet. From there we'll determine when you can go home," she says. "Get some rest. I'll be in a little later to check on you."

"Thank you, Doctor," Myra adds as Dr. Fletcher leaves.

———

THE NEXT MORNING is possibly one of the most humbling days of my life. Sponge bath (they're afraid I won't be able to stand long enough in the shower), more poking and prodding, and finally, removing the catheter—once I was deemed okay enough to walk to the toilet to pee. I still need to sit once I'm there. Standing privileges come for those who don't need a walker to get around.

With all that went on today, I'm exhausted by the time Emma stops in after work.

"Are you okay?" she asks, noting how defeated I look.

"I'm fine. Just a long day."

"Is this a bad time?"

Chapter Two

"No!" I blurt. "I need to talk to someone who isn't here just to invade my personal space."

She laughs and I do too.

"Cale told me you were awake. Sorry I didn't stop in yesterday. By the time I got out of work, it was past the visiting hours. He said that your parents were here, though. That's good."

"Yeah. They want me to transfer out to New Haven, but that's not going to happen."

"Then I'd really never see you! I've been making sure someone was here every day so you wouldn't be alone."

I grin. "Thanks, Emma."

She grasps my hand but pulls away quickly. "You shocked me!"

I raise an eyebrow. "It's too soon for shocking jokes. I'm still laid up."

She reaches for my hand again but stops before she touches me. "They took off your bandages."

I look down at my right arm. I'm sporting new body art: a dark red line reaches from my fingertips up my arm, with several smaller lines branching off in different directions.

"Pretty cool, huh? It was a minor burn from the strike. It's still a little tender, but otherwise it's fine."

"Will that heal?" she asks.

I shake my head. "I don't think so."

"At least you get a badass battle scar from this whole thing," she says. Her fingers graze the mark. "Your own lightning bolt to remember all of this."

"Apparently Tranidek Energy wants to pay for my medical bills."

"Really? That's odd."

"I know."

"No, I mean, you're already all over the news as it is. I wonder why Tranidek stepped in."

"It sounds like they might want to hire me."

She grins. "But you have a job."

"Yeah. Hopefully I don't have any issues with the time I'm taking off, though."

She shakes her head. "You won't."

"So . . . I'm on the news?"

"Oh yeah. It's not every day someone is struck down by lighting *indoors*." She shakes her head and chuckles. "You won't let anyone one-up you, will you?"

"Guess not." We're quiet for a minute, and then I remember why I worked so late at the office to begin with. "Hey, what ever happened at that meeting with Marble?"

"Oh. That." She reaches back and runs her fingers through her blonde hair, swinging some of it around on her shoulder.

"Did he fire you?" I pull up the blankets and pretend to step out—knowing full well that I'd be on my face in a minute after the day I've had. "I'm gonna go kick someone's ass!"

She puts her hands up to stop me. "No! He didn't fire me." She tries to help me back into bed, but I'm already settled. The IV hooked into my arm wouldn't have let me go anywhere anyway.

"Good, 'cause I would've told them I'm not coming in until you're back at IT tech support with the best of us." She doesn't smile, and my expression changes. "What happened, Em?"

"I'm not at IT tech support anymore."

Chapter Three

She tucks her hair behind her ear and looks at our inter-twined fingers.

"Did you get transferred to the plant?" My mouth is dry and I wonder if she got fired after all, but it doesn't make sense.

"I'm the IT manager. He gave me Henry Haney's old job."

I stare at her. "So you're my boss?"

"Guess so." Her eyes wander up from our hands, along my scar until they finally meet my eyes.

"That's great, Emma! Congratulations!" I smile and reach for her hand again, but she pulls away. Another shock.

"You're not mad?"

"Why would I be mad?"

She cocks her head to the side. "Ethan, we're both equally qualified, and yet he still chose me."

"Well, if you put it that way . . . " I flash my teeth again. "No really, it's fine. With the way things are nowadays, I'm just happy we both still have jobs—I *do* still have a job, right?"

"The good thing about being your boss is that I have a say in your job security. As far as I'm concerned, you're still employed."

Her face scrunches as a thought hits her. "Unless there's some rule I'm forgetting. Or Mr. Marble wants you gone . . . then it's kind of out of my hands. Sorry."

I chuckle. "I'm sure I'll be fine."

"Yeah, you have a couple weeks' recovery anyway."

A knock on the door breaks our conversation. It's Dr. Fletcher. "Excuse me, may I have a word with Mr. Pierce in private?"

"Oh, sure!" Emma snatches up her purse from the side of her chair, then leans down and kisses my cheek. "Um . . . I'll see you later."

When she leaves, Dr. Fletcher pulls the chart from the end of my bed and scans it over. "She's cute. Girlfriend?"

"Yeah. When do you think I'll be able to go home?"

"Well, the physical therapist was satisfied with how you walked today. But he still wants you to do PT for a bit outside of here. If all goes well, I don't see why you wouldn't be able to go home tomorrow or the day after." Her eyes flit over the clipboard and she adds, "So long as you take it easy."

"Of course. What about work?" I can't help but think about how the lack of income is hurting Cale. Our rent isn't cheap, living near Chester Park and all.

"I would advise you to wait a couple weeks." She drops the chart back in the holder at the foot of my bed and slips her hands in the pockets of her white lab coat. "You were electrocuted, Mr. Pierce. You were exposed to a very high amount of voltage. Most people wouldn't have survived that. To be honest, I'm actually a little surprised that you did."

I let out a huff of air. "Thanks for telling it straight."

She nods to my arm. "I hope that scar reminds you of how lucky you are. Think about how tired you feel now. With a full work week, that amount would be tripled. You may even end up back in the hospital. Take it easy for a few weeks. Relax. Stay at home. Catch up on TV or a book or something."

I give her a thumbs-up. "Got it."

She pulls out a piece of paper from her pocket and hands it to me. I unfold it and see a phone number scribbled on it. Is she hitting on me?

CHAPTER THREE

"On a more personal note," she continues, "This is actually my last week at the hospital. I would like you to consider coming for weekly check-ups to the clinic I'm opening in Hopman."

Nope, definitely not hitting on me. My cheeks grow hot.

"I want to continue to monitor your recovery," she says. "Like I said, you took a high amount of voltage, and I want to be sure your heart is still able to hold up two, three, four weeks from now. We'll reduce your visits on a conditional basis."

Refolding the paper, I ask, "You think there's something wrong with my heart?"

"Not necessarily." She sighs and shifts her weight onto her other foot. "We needed to resuscitate you three times. That takes a toll on your body. I just want to make sure everything holds up. And, if I can be frank again, I'm curious."

"So I'd have to go down to Hopman?" My mind flashes to the numerous news reports Cale does from down there. Murders, drug busts, even a couple kidnappings.

She looks to the floor for a moment. "I know it's not the best neighborhood, but I'd like to do my part for those who need it. Opening a clinic will provide much-needed support for that area of the city. But if you don't feel comfortable coming down there, I understand. I can make arrangements with another doctor for your follow-up care. I just wanted to give you my number in case you were interested. I'm still putting together my team and haven't quite set up my office yet, so I have no way to make appointments."

I consider the idea of going down to the worst part of the city on a regular basis. My parents would flip out. So would Cale and Emma, although I doubt Emma would directly tell me not to. She knows me by now. You tell me not to do something, and it's the exact thing I'm going to do.

Still, it makes me nervous. But it's only once a week, and it'll be during the day. I'll be fine. Just stick to the main streets.

"You can think it over a bit and weigh your options," she adds.

I shake my head. "No, it's fine. I'll come. Sign me up."

FUSE: ORIGIN

———

THE NEXT MORNING I wake up in my own apartment. Cale has already left for work—down at WOPA, the television news station—and everything is quiet.

He called a cab last night when he brought me home so we could avoid the subway. By the time we got up to our apartment, I was wiped. I collapsed on the recliner and didn't move until . . . well, I haven't moved yet.

I pull out my phone from my back pocket—my butt is numb from sleeping on it—and notice my battery is at 1 percent. I ignore the dying device and check out what's on Facebook. Emma added her new job to her profile, but her most recent posts are updates about me. I read through some of the comments, wishing me well, offering Emma condolences. Twenty minutes later, I see that my phone is now up to 78 percent. Weird.

I toss it on the coffee table and get up slowly. I'm tired, but I smell from having gone a week without proper bathing.

When I get out of the shower, I'm ready to sit down again. It's just a shower stall, and we don't have a bench or even a railing in there. I was afraid I was going to fall a couple times.

I collapse in the recliner again and reach for the remote. When I point it to turn the TV on, the screen sparks and then cuts out. I notice a flicker of white lightning rolling across my fingertips. I drop the remote and stare at my hands until it subsides.

My heart beating faster now, I snatch my phone from the coffee table and scroll through for Dr. Fletcher's number. Instantly it surges to 100 percent. I find her entry and hit "Send."

I get her away message and bite my thumbnail as I wait for the beep.

"Dr. Fletcher! It's Ethan Pierce. I, uh . . . I think I need to bump up my appointment. Something weird—just call me back when you get this!"

I click off the phone, but my shaky hands can't hold on, and it tumbles to the floor. Tremors rack my body. A warm feeling spreads throughout my limbs, and I suddenly can't keep my

Chapter Three

hands still. I feel like I want to scream or run, anything to get a sense of release.

I stand and walk to the window. I smell the smoke from the TV shorting out and open the window for fresh air. I tap my hands against the windowsill, desperate to keep them moving.

My phone begins to buzz on the hardwood floor and I jump, sending a bright streak of white lighting surging across the street to the neighboring building.

I stare wide-eyed at my hand, awestruck. The tremors have stopped and the warmth diffuses. A black mark smudges the red-brick wall of the building, and I catch a wave of smoke rising from the mark on the opposite building before the wind whisks it away.

I pick up my phone and answer it just before it goes to voice-mail.

"Mr. Pierce?" It's Dr. Fletcher. "What's the matter? You sounded anxious on your message."

I gulp and think about the best way to explain what just happened without sounding crazy. "Um . . . I think something weird is happening to me. I don't know how to describe it."

"Weird how?"

"You won't believe it."

"Try me."

"I just shot lightning across the street!"

She's quiet for a moment. I shake my head, feeling like an idiot for saying something so stupid. She must think I'm hallucinating. She's going to put me in the psychiatric center, and I'm going to spend the rest of my life eating applesauce with the guy who thinks he's Elvis Presley reincarnated.

Her voice snaps me out of my moment of paranoia.

"Can someone bring you to the clinic? I took the day off to put together the office, but I'll make time for you."

Cale, Emma, or even Myra. Those are my only three choices. All three would give me grief for going down to Hopman. All three have jobs. The only one I might be able to bug is Emma. She's also the least likely to make me feel even more stupid for thinking I just shot lightning out my window.

FUSE: ORIGIN

"I might be able to ask someone," I finally say.

"Okay good." She gives me the address and I scribble it down on the front of an old pizza box—tucked between the garbage can and the counter—Cale's idea of making dinner and cleaning up.

"I'll wait until you show up. *Do not* bring yourself."

I nod and then add a moment later, "Yes."

"Hopefully I'll see you shortly, Mr. Pierce. Call me if something comes up."

————

"YOU DID WHAT, exactly?" Emma asks as we roll up to a stoplight along Wilkinson Avenue—a main street that runs south through the city to the skeevy Hopman neighborhood. We just passed out of the construction zone for the solar roadway installation, which had traffic backed up in all directions.

"I told you it was weird."

Emma didn't hesitate when I told her I needed a ride to see Dr. Fletcher. Didn't ask any questions, either, until we were in the car and she was sure I was okay. Well, as okay as I can be for someone who's hallucinating. Even now, as I explain what happened, she's trying to rationalize it.

"So you think the accident gave you supernatural powers?" She fixes her glasses and continues on to the next stoplight. "I didn't realize you were a comic book nerd."

"That's not what I said—"

"It's basically what you said," she interjects. "I mean, I think it's cool. You know, as long as this isn't you tripping on some new medication or anything."

"It's not—" I stop before I can finish. I don't even know if what I saw was real or not. Maybe there *was* a slip-up in the drugs I was given at the hospital. Maybe these are withdrawal symptoms.

We pull up to the address, but Emma leaves the car running.

"Uh . . . are you sure this is the place?" she asks.

The buildings around us are mostly abandoned. They're

20

CHAPTER THREE

littered with graffiti and trash. There's a group of people standing outside of a corner store, one of the few open businesses on the block. They all stop and stare at us as we idle. One woman, with part of her hair tightly braided against her head, gives a scowl when I catch her eye.

The building that's supposedly Dr. Fletcher's could use a fresh coat of paint itself, but otherwise it's a gem compared to its neighbors.

"I don't know," I say. "I don't see any other car here. She said she'd be here."

"Maybe she was murdered," Emma mutters as she looks around.

"Not funny, Em."

"What about that driveway? Where does that go?" Before I can answer, she's following the strip of potholed pavement that leads behind the building. One lone car sits in the small parking lot. It doesn't look like it's spent any time at a scrapyard, which fills me with hope that it's Dr. Fletcher's.

We approach the door and knock on it nervously, wondering what we're getting ourselves into. When it swings open, both of us jump.

"You made it!" Dr. Fletcher meets us at the door. She's not wearing her white lab coat. Instead, she's in a pair of jeans and an old concert T-shirt.

"Hey, nice tee!" Emma says. I shoot her a look and she says, "Sorry."

Dr. Fletcher tugs at her T-shirt. "Yeah, I'm sorry about all this. It's a work in progress." She spreads her arms and motions around the room. Only a few of the fluorescent lights are on, and the front desk is piled high with papers. Stacks of chairs line the hallways, and various machines provide obstacles as we maneuver through the clinic. "What's going on? You sounded worried on the phone."

"He's got magic now!" Emma blurts. I shoot her another look. "Sorry. I'll give you guys a minute." She flashes a smile and wanders off toward a large white machine in the next room and pretends to look interested.

21

Fuse: Origin

Dr. Fletcher smiles.

"Look, I know what she said sounds crazy, but that's really what happened," I say. She opens her mouth to reply, but I put up my hand to stop her. "I know. It's probably some side effect or something causing an illusion. Are there any new meds I can take so I don't hallucinate anymore?"

"Mr. Pierce—"

"Call me Ethan. You've seen me comatose. Crazy can't be much worse."

She leans against the front desk and looks at me. "I don't think you're crazy. It's quite possible you're generating some static electricity. You may have shocked yourself and seen a spark. Couple that with your first day back from the hospital, and you may have thought you saw the spark shoot across the street."

"There are scorch marks on the next building!" I pull out my phone and show her a picture. "Zoom in, you can see it."

She pinches the screen and lifts it closer to her face. "Are you sure that's not just dirt?"

"Dr. Fletcher—"

"Alex." She offers a smile.

"Alex," I repeat, "this isn't static electricity. I don't think I'm . . . supernatural or whatever, but I do think there's more happening here."

She brings her hands together, entwining her fingers. "Well, I'd certainly be interested in looking into the possibility that something else is going on here. As long as you'd be willing to be a subject."

"Like a lab rat?"

She shrugs. "It'd be research, yes. But believe me when I say what we do with the results will be completely up to you."

I've been standing too long and I feel exhausted. Alex notices this and pulls a chair from a stack in the corner and sets it down. She wraps an arm around me and grabs my arm to help me into the chair. It's unnecessary but nice.

"Are you okay?" she asks.

"What's going on?" Emma comes to my side.

"I'm fine. Just tired."

Chapter Three

"You should probably get him back home," Alex tells her.

She nods. "I'll pull up the car."

When she's gone, I turn to Alex. "Call me when you're ready to start."

CHAPTER FOUR

So you're the lightning boy," my physical therapist says. It's my first time here. Apparently the therapist I saw at the hospital only works with patients who are admitted. Dr. Fletcher—Alex—recommended Dean Adams to me.

He's dressed almost like a gym teacher in windbreaker pants and an Under Armour polo, and he's jacked.

"Is that going to be my legacy now?"

He turns his hands palms up. "Hey, you're the one who managed to get struck by lightning. Eat it up while you can." He smiles and offers his hand. "I'm Dean Adams."

"Ethan Pierce."

We both flinch when our hands touch. Another static shock.

He holds on to my hand and turns my arm to examine my scar. "Now that's cool."

"You should get one," I kid.

"And steal your thunder?" He flashes me a smile and we both laugh at his pun.

Dean asks if I have any pain or weakness, which I do, and

Chapter Four

he gives me different exercises and massages to do to build my strength back up.

"Basically, you have to reteach your muscles how to work," he explains between exercises. "It's like the lightning hit a reset button on your body and you have to start all over again."

"Sounds exhausting just thinking about it."

"At least you still have basic motor skills. Some lightning-strike patients have to relearn how to talk or swallow. Other people have cognitive or hearing issues. Or they just lose all feeling in parts of their body. All in all, your symptoms are pretty mild. Dr. Fletcher said that her biggest concern for you is your heart."

After hooking up a few cords to my chest, he has me walk on the treadmill at various speeds. Nothing too strenuous, but still, I'm exhausted by the time the appointment is over.

This is the first time I've realized the full extent of my limitations, and it's frustrating. I can barely walk half a mile without getting winded.

"You'll get there," he reassures me. "You just need to build up your strength again."

"I feel like such an idiot."

"I know. But really, you're doing great. It's only your first day! Baby steps. Before you know it, you'll be running."

Now I laugh. "Yeah, like I ever ran before."

———

IT'S BEEN THREE weeks since I agreed to be Alex's lab rat. Almost every day I've been going down to the clinic to have some tests run. It's perfect since I'm on leave from work. Between my trips to the clinic and to PT with Dean, I've also been looking into Tranidek more and considering the offer. I actually applied to work there right after I graduated college, but that was when Wyatt bought out Tranidek's solar roadway contract and they had a mass hiring event. Wyatt was the superior choice at the time.

Mr. Rizzoli's job offer seems too good to be true. How will I know I have job security? How will I know the compensation will be the same? The benefits package? That I'll even like what I'm doing? I know nothing about the position they have in mind for me—if that's even what Mr. Rizzoli implied in his letter. I'd need to hear more details before I'd even consider any offer. My job at Wyatt might not be the most exciting, but it's stable. I've done it for a few years now, and I'm comfortable—in my position and with my finances.

Regardless, I wrote a letter thanking Mr. Rizzoli for his generosity for paying my medical bills. At the very least, I owe him that. It's not like I ever considered turning down his money, because God knows I couldn't afford those bills. The health insurance through Wyatt isn't *that* good.

My phone begins to buzz, breaking me out of my train of thought. I see Alex's name displayed on the screen.

"This is Ethan," I say when I answer. I just fixed myself a sandwich for lunch and am still standing at the counter. I've been getting stronger. The exercises Dean has me doing have been working.

"Ethan, I've got the latest test results from your blood and they're . . . interesting. We should discuss them in person," she says.

That makes me a little nervous. After three weeks of blood tests, urine tests, EKGs, CTs, X-rays, and other tests, all of my results have been coming back fairly normal—at least for a guy who was recently struck by lightning and hospitalized. Not anything a mutant with lightning powers would have.

"Sure. I'll be over in an hour or so."

"Be careful getting here."

Much to everyone's objections, I've been taking the subway to the clinic and to PT. It's just been too much of a hassle to arrange a ride with someone. They all have jobs and can't exactly pick me up in the middle of the day to chauffeur me around the city. Besides, it gets me out of the house and keeps me from going stir crazy. And I figure getting a few extra steps in each day can't hurt.

Cale, Emma, and especially Alex all think I'm risking a heart attack anytime I stand up for longer than five minutes. The truth of the matter is, I feel fine. My heart races occasionally—usually around the time I get a surge. Whether it's actually static electricity or not is yet to be determined. Based off the tests Alex has run, my body could still be dehydrated from the incident, causing static shocks. But nothing's conclusive.

The only thing that really bothers me about my trip to Hopman is the three-block walk from the subway station to the clinic. Despite my attempts not to stand out, I've gotten several shifty glances. Maybe that's why my heart races.

"I'll be fine, Alex," I reply to her on the phone. "I've done this a thousand times by now."

She sighs. "Otherwise, how are you feeling? How's PT going?"

"Slow, but Dean says I'm getting there. After each session I'm not as tired as I was when we first started."

"Well that's good. Sounds like you're recovering well."

"Yeah, I thought so until you said something weird came up in one of my tests."

"Try not to worry about it. That won't help anything. I'll see you soon."

———

SOMETHING'S DIFFERENT TODAY on my walk from the subway to the clinic. Besides my usual apprehension walking in this neighborhood, something feels off. Even though most days I try to avoid meeting anyone's eyes, I usually notice the occasional person. But today there's no one around.

It's as if all life in Hopman has completely stopped. The roar of the cars whizzing by on the expressway is the only sound. The only sign of life I see are a few faces peeking out from behind makeshift curtains. Kids, mostly, but a few adults as well.

Being a well-dressed white man in this part of the city puts a large target on my back—especially now that I'm the only one on the street. I pick up the pace and hurry inside the doors of the clinic.

The place actually looks like a doctor's office now. The front desk has file organizers and a new computer. The floors shine with fresh wax, and the halls smell of potpourri trying to cover the smell of fresh paint. The fluorescent lights make the whole place shine. It doesn't look like it belongs in a place like Hopman, but it sure has Olympia's renaissance written all over it.

The receptionist sits behind the front desk with the phone pressed to her ear and an open folder in front of her. The waiting room has a few patients watching the news on the TV anchored to the wall in the corner.

Alex comes out of the room adjacent to the front desk and greets me. A man steps out behind her. He's wearing a black scrub top and jeans. He extends his hand to me, and I shake it.

"Ethan, I'd like you to meet Dr. Wesley Strider," Alex says. "He's one of the doctors who helped me start the clinic."

"Wes," he says, squeezing my hand tight. From the salt-and-pepper hair and few wrinkles around his eyes, he looks to be about my parents' age.

Alex leads us into an empty room and closes the door behind us. "He's a friend of mine who I've consulted with on this case," she explains. "He was one of my professors at OU. He's a brilliant doctor, specializing in transmutations."

"Transmutations?" I ask. My mind immediately flickers to the X-Men, but I keep that bit to myself.

"When Dr. Fletcher told me about your condition, I immediately thought of a mutation of sorts." He reaches for my right arm and I lift it for him. His fingers trace the lightning mark as he talks. "Your body seems to have adapted pretty well to the shock. It got me wondering about what happened while you were comatose."

Alex cocks her head to the computer. "Why don't we show you what we found?"

Wes lets me have my arm back, and I take a seat on a swivel stool near one of the counters. He takes a seat by a microscope and looks through it.

"Alex, the lights please?"

Once it's dark, the image from the microscope is displayed against the white wall.

Chapter Four

"What exactly am I looking at?" I ask. The image is fuzzy, but it looks like a diagram you'd see in a high school biology class.

"These are some of your cells taken from your blood sample," Wes explains. He looks into the eyepiece of the microscope again, scrunching up his top lip as he focuses the image with a new level of magnification. He looks up at the screen before continuing.

"Okay, do you see here?" He points with a laser pointer. "Do you see the way this is moving so rapidly?"

I squint, trying to see the image through a scientist's eyes. "Yeah, I guess."

"Your cells have four times the energy of anyone else's." He returns to the microscope and pulls the slide away, replacing it with another one. Again, his lip curls up as he focuses the image. "Here, this is a sample of my own blood cells. Note the speed at which they're moving."

I gape for a moment. His cells appear stationary in comparison. "So what does this mean?"

"Before we answer that, let me show you one more slide," he says.

Another image is up on the wall. The pieces move much faster than the previous two slides.

"What is that?" I ask.

"The sample we took just before you experienced one of your electric . . . events," Alex responds.

I squint my eyes again, trying to figure out which question to ask first.

"Mr. Pierce," Wes starts, "you said you feel moments of . . . " he wiggles his fingers as he thinks of the correct word, " . . . restlessness, correct?"

I nod. "Yeah, it's like I'm constantly in danger of shocking myself." I decide to leave off the horrible bedhead I've been getting and, oh yeah, the few times I've shot lighting out of my hands. That's happened several times. I guess the term is "electric event" now.

Alex has now seen one of these events firsthand. I left scorch marks on her newly painted walls. She knows I'm not lying.

Fuse: Origin

"No previous diagnosis of ADD or ADHD?" Wes continues. I shake my head no.

"Tell me more about these electric events."

I shrug. "It only happens sometimes. I still think it's just static—"

"It is *not* static electricity!" he shouts in excitement. "Static electricity, while you do see the occasional spark now and then, does not have the power behind it to leave marks on walls. Not only that, but Dr. Fletcher says that you shot it across the street? That is certainly not the work of static electricity." His eyes light up with intrigue.

I shrug. "So what's wrong with me? Why am I suddenly my own power plant?"

Wes holds up a finger and leans closer. "My theory is that when you were electrocuted in your office, your body wasn't damaged by the charge but instead mutated to accommodate it. Think of the coma as a caterpillar's cocoon."

"Then tell me," I pull up the sleeve of my shirt, "what this is! This is from the strike. I was in a coma for a week. Alex says that my heart stopped—multiple times! I've spent the last few weeks trying to build up my strength again. I think I've been pretty badly damaged."

"Ethan!" Alex stops me. "Your body was certainly damaged, but what Wes is trying to say is that other than your initial responses to the strike, you don't suffer from any long-term damage. An electrocution of that magnitude is potentially fatal. Not only were you struck by the lightning, but your body was also exposed to the power running through the entire building. Most victims have lifelong effects from a strike that strong. You are lucky."

"I'm *lucky*?" I say, disgusted. "I'm constantly shocking people! I can't touch anything electrical without wondering if I'm going to blow a fuse or kill myself if I take a shower!" I stand and walk to the door.

"Mr. Pierce, I believe that you may be able to learn how to control this ability. Think of the possibilities," Wes says with wonder in his eyes. "The city is already heading into a renaissance with alternative energy. Imagine if the world discovered that man could also generate it."

"If you think this is such an opportunity, maybe you should've been the one to get struck by lightning," I say as I reach for the door. A small spark arcs between my fingertips and the metal doorknob. I groan in frustration.

"Ethan, we can help you through this," Alex says.

"Just give me time to think." Ignoring the second spark when I reach for the door, I walk out and back to the street.

I shouldn't have yelled at Alex and Wes like that. It's not their fault I was electrocuted. I guess it's just human nature to let out your anger at the bearer of bad news.

And what bad news it is. Not only is my body permanently scarred, but now I've also mutated? So shocking people all the time is just a part of my charm now, apparently. And what do I do if it's not just a little shock? What if I strike someone down with a big bolt of lightning? How am I supposed to function like a normal person if I'm afraid to touch anyone?

Thunder rumbles in the distance, and I look up to see the ominous sky over the city. I sigh as I hurry toward the subway station. I wish I'd never been struck by lightning.

———

THE NEXT DAY I'm at Wyatt Industries' solar panel manufacturing plant in Hopman for an interview with the *Olympia Tribune*. With as many times as the reporter called me, I agreed just to get her to stop. Of course, when we set up the interview, the only time she had available was early evening.

Even though I've never actually worked at the plant—never even been here at all—she said that getting pictures with solar panels would be a better scene than in a bland office. Perhaps this is how the media twists stories?

"Ethan Pierce, the boy who was struck by lightning," Bebe Hawkins, says when we sit down in the break room of the plant. She seems perfectly comfortable, but I hold my hands in my lap with my shoulders tucked in. She leans back in her chair and crosses one leg over the other in her black skirt.

"You must feel pretty lucky for having such a quick recovery," she starts.

Lucky. There's that word again.

"It hasn't been easy, and I'm still working on it, but I guess I've come a long way in a short time."

My PT sessions have become easier. Dean's begun to push me harder. Walking faster, lifting more weights. It's probably the most intense workout I've had since high school gym class.

Bebe and I talk for a good hour. I tell her about my recovery and what I remember from that day. She keeps trying to find an angle, but after a while I'm afraid of the one she's going to use: average guy has something extraordinary happen to him. The peak in my endlessly mundane life.

"Let's see if we can get some pictures outside." She holds the door open for me, and we head through the cavernous warehouse. She rambles about something—I think the solar panels on her building—but I don't hear over the roar of the machines. Once she finds a spot worthy enough, she tries to get me to relax. I'm not used to being the center of attention, and I hate it. My arms hang at my sides and my shoulders slump.

"Okay, why don't you put your good arm on your hip and hold the one with your scar out so I can get that," she suggests.

My *good* arm?

I do what she says and then she directs me into a few other poses, snapping more pictures, further increasing my anxiety.

"Well, I think that's everything I need." She fastens the lens cap back in place and extends her hand. "I'll give you a call if I have any follow-up questions."

I hesitate before shaking her hand and, sure enough, she jumps at the static shock.

"You're just a lightning machine, now, aren't you?" she says with a giggle.

I pretend to laugh, and we move toward the exit.

"Your story is truly amazing," she tells me again as she hooks her thumb on the strap of her bag. "To think, nobody knew your name until that bolt of lightning struck your building. And the fact that the love of your life found you sprawled out on the floor. Oh, the things that must've been going through her mind!"

Another forced smile spreads across my face.

"My editor wasn't sure who to assign to this story, but I told him just how incredible it is and he finally let me do it." She waves her free hand around as she talks. "I just love doing stories like this!"

My phone starts to buzz in my back pocket and I breathe a sigh of relief at the excuse. I don't recognize the number, but there's no way I'm not answering it. Having walked into another section of the plant, the noise of the machines running has died away a bit.

I stop where I am and tell Bebe, "Excuse me, I should take this."

"Oh, of course." She shakes my hand again. "Thanks for everything, Ethan."

"Ethan Pierce," I answer when she turns to head toward the door.

"This is Joe Gotti," a husky voice on the other end says.

I slowly move toward the exit again, not wanting to catch up to Bebe. "Hi. What can I do for you?"

"I work at Tranidek Energy. I'm Frank Rizzoli's personal assistant."

I nod. "Right. Okay. It's very generous of you guys to pay my medical bills. I definitely wasn't expecting that since I work for Wyatt." How ironic to get a call from someone at Tranidek while in Wyatt's plant.

He lets out a huff of air and I can almost hear his smile. "That was Mr. Rizzoli's decision. That's actually why I'm calling, actually. He really would like to speak with you personally."

All I can do is nod. I've never even met most of the executives at Wyatt. What would it look like if I was seen being chummy with the guys at Tranidek?

"Just a conversation," he continues. "Consider it your thanks for the check he's about to write to FOMC. He has an opening next week, Thursday at six. Does that work for you?"

"Uh, sure. Yeah, okay." I reach the exit and stop under a streetlight.

FUSE: ORIGIN

"Great. Let me give you our address," he says.

"It's okay. I can look it up online."

"All right, then. When you come in, just tell the men at the front desk that you have an appointment with Mr. Rizzoli and they'll direct you to his office. If you have any problems, give me a call back."

"Okay, thank you."

I stand on the sidewalk outside the plant long after he's hung up and look up where their office is on my phone. Out in Midtown. I could probably see their building from the rooftop of mine.

"Ethan?"

I spin around and see Emma.

She giggles and asks, "What are you doing here? Crap, was today interview day?"

"Yeah. What are *you* doing here?"

"I just came back from an IT meeting that ran late. Sorry, I completely forgot about your interview. I meant to stop in to say hi."

After I lean in for a kiss, I say, "Don't worry about it."

I lead us toward the subway on Hopkins Boulevard. The whole street has a different feel in the dark. The boarded-up buildings, graffiti, and unwelcoming industrial warehouses make my heart pump a little faster. I know exactly why this is the perfect hunting ground for criminals.

"I'll make you dinner tonight to make it up to you."

I smile. "Well, I'd be stupid to turn that down." We walk for a moment in comfortable silence. "I just got invited to talk to the CEO of Tranidek."

"The one who's paying your medical bills?"

"Yeah."

"What does he want to talk to you about?"

I shrug. "I have no idea. His personal assistant just called me after the interview and told me to consider it my thanks for the big ol' check Tranidek's writing."

"Wow."

"Yeah. This isn't going to hurt my job at Wyatt, is it?"

Chapter Four

"Well . . . it could. Tranidek is trying to cash in on your accident and issued a press release announcing they're paying for your bills. Wyatt's board of trustees isn't happy with that. I guess some people think you should've turned down the offer. Said worker's compensation would've helped cover the bills."

"And take forever to get it all taken care of? No thanks."

"I know. I'm just the messenger."

"How do they even know I accepted?" I just mailed the letter to Mr. Rizzoli yesterday. There's no way he got it in time to issue a press release. Especially not one that would be on the agenda for the latest board meeting.

"The press release went out last week. I guess since you never denied the money, Tranidek assumed you accepted." She shrugs. "Then again, why wouldn't you accept it? It's not like Wyatt was jumping up to pay for you."

"Right?" I mutter.

"When you go to this meeting, you just need to present yourself as someone who is representing Wyatt. No harm in that."

"Right. If Wyatt has a problem with it, hopefully I can reassure them that I'm not looking to jump ship."

"Exactly!"

We walk quietly for a minute longer before I change the subject. "So I meant to tell you that I talked to Dr. Fletcher yesterday."

"Yeah? What did she find?"

"A second doctor."

"Really? Don't you need to sign off on that or something?"

I shrug. "It's research. It's probably okay. I don't care that much. Anyway, the best he could come up with is that my body mutated and basically now I can shoot lightning out of my hands spontaneously."

"So what we already knew?"

"Basically," I continue.

"So who is this second doctor? What're they like?"

"Wesley Strider. Thinks I've been given some kind of a gift."

"Hmm. Too bad you can't control it. Then Wyatt would be paying you for a different reason," Emma tries to joke. Her eyes shift to the attention she's getting from the homeless men across the street. They're calling to her and commenting on her formfitting blue dress and black heels.

I wrap my arm around her, and we pick up our pace. I feel vulnerable, but I force myself to keep talking. Act like everything is okay for her sake.

"He actually thinks I can learn to control it, but I don't know—"

The screech of tires on the pavement cuts me off. A black SUV barrels down the street. I pull Emma to the ground and we huddle against the nearest building as rapid-fire gunshots fill the air behind us. I cover her with my body and don't look up.

My heart pounds in my chest. I wonder how long we'll lie here before someone reports our bodies to the police. How will Cale and my parents be? First the lightning strike, now this.

Emma shakes beneath me. My hands are clamped down on her arms, pinning her in place to cover her as much as I can.

After what feels like an eternity, the shots stop.

"Are you okay?" I mutter to Emma.

She nods and looks over my shoulder.

With my ears ringing, I turn and catch sight of the driver. Dark, slicked-back hair. Round face and eyes that squint when he flashes his yellow teeth. The car slows and the man moves to get out, but police sirens go off in the distance, and instead, he just points to us. We can see the men in the back seat move, and I'm afraid we're going to get a gun shoved in our faces. The driver holds his gaze with us for a moment until the car speeds down the street with another screech of the tires.

"You okay?" I ask Emma again.

She nods and I help her stand.

Across the street I see a man lying on the ground. The homeless men have scattered. I'm grateful for that. I run across the street to check on him but stop before I even reach the sidewalk.

The brick wall behind him is splattered in his blood. Even more is pooled around his body. I turn away when I spot pieces of his flesh scattered around him.

When Emma joins me she lets out a scream that is drowned out by the police cars approaching.

CHAPTER FIVE

The policemen hop out of their cars, wielding their guns. One of them approaches me and Emma.

"Are you hurt?" he asks.

I shake my head no and look to Emma. She mimics me.

He nods. "Good. We'll need to get your statements—"

The voice on his radio cuts him off. "Scene's clear. Tuck's almost here."

"Detective Cross is going to want to ask you some questions when he gets here," the officer says. Officer Raymond, according to the tag on his uniform.

I wrap my arm around Emma to reassure her and watch as another car pulls up before the scene is sectioned off.

"Ethan Pierce," Tucker Cross says as he steps out of the car. He's a stocky black man who used to intimidate the shit out of me when I was younger. He and Cale were best friends in high school. They fell out of touch after college. I haven't seen him in years.

"Are you okay?" he asks. "What are you doing way out here?" He turns to Officer Raymond. "I've got it, thanks."

FUSE: ORIGIN

Tucker shakes my hand but jerks away at my touch. Another shock.

"We're fine," I say quickly, "just . . . you know."

"Yeah, I know." He nods. "This your girlfriend?" Emma's hand is gripping mine like a vice.

"Yeah, this is Emma."

He offers her his hand and she shakes it too. "So what happened?" He's in detective mode now.

"We were walking to the subway when this SUV came out of nowhere and started shooting."

The other officers who arrived before Tucker are snapping pictures, taking samples, and radioing for a coroner.

"Did you get a good look at them? Driver, gunman, anyone?"

I look to Emma. She chokes out, "Yeah. And he saw us."

"Who?"

"The driver," I say.

"What about the vehicle? Anything identifiable about it? Color, scratches, bumper stickers? Anything?"

I shrug. "Black SUV-type. Didn't see what the make or model was."

Tucker sighs. "Did you get a look at the plates?" He looks at Emma now.

She shakes her head vigorously.

"Where were you guys coming from?"

"We both work at Wyatt," I respond.

Officer Raymond returns to whisper something to Tucker.

I look down the street as an ambulance pulls up. I focus my attention on the building we're standing in front of. It looks like it used to be an elegant theater. Now its front doors are covered with plywood.

"This area of the city has really spiraled out of control, hasn't it?" I ask when Raymond returns to the other officers.

Tucker huffs a laugh. "You have no idea."

"It looks like it's got good bones," Emma adds. Her voice seems to be returning, though she's still clinging to my hand like life support. "Why don't more people try to do more with it?"

Chapter Five

Tucker shakes his head. "The residents aren't the problem. Now," he says, ending the conversation, "I need to get each of your statements officially." He glances at our intertwined hands. "Separately."

Emma nods and lets go.

"You're welcome to wait in my car if that'll make you feel better," he adds.

"No, I'll be fine." She walks toward the police cars parked on the street.

He records my official witness statement and I sign off on it before I trade places with Emma and Tucker gets hers. It's all formality. I know Tucker trusts our word, but he needs something on paper for his files. It also gives us a chance to give more details about the driver.

When Emma's done, they both come over to where I'm standing. It's getting late.

"I suggest you both steer clear of this area," he says. "As you've seen tonight, there are some dangerous people in this city."

"Next time I'm at the plant, I'm calling a cab," Emma mutters.

Tucker gives me a tight smile and slaps my arm again. "Thanks, man. Listen, me, you, and your brother should have a beer sometime. He still in town?"

"Yep." I reach for my stinging shoulder. "We actually live by Chester Park."

"No kidding! I'll have to give you guys a call. Do you need a ride home?"

I look down at Emma. The subway is only one block away, but I know she just wants to get out of here as soon as possible. "If you wouldn't mind."

"Sure thing. I'll have one of my guys take you. You can wait in my car if you'd prefer."

In the back of Tucker's sedan, I can feel Emma shaking beside me. I wrap my arm around her and pull her close. It's only in the quiet of the car that I realize my heart is racing as if I ran a hundred miles.

Fuse: Origin

EMMA'S HANDS ARE ice cold when we get back to her apartment. We wordlessly agreed that I'd stay here tonight. It's closer than my place, and I don't want to leave her alone. The look in Emma's eyes makes me want to do whatever it takes to give her a sense of security.

The first thing she does when we get in is fill two glasses with wine. The way my nerves are, I'd prefer vodka, but anything will help. I've been shocking her at every touch since it happened. A direct result of my nerves, I'm sure.

She follows my gaze and says, "I thought we could both use a drink, and wine was the only thing I had." She hands me mine and takes a gulp of hers.

She leads me to the couch, and we clink our glasses together. "To one hell of a night. May we never relive it again."

"I will definitely drink to that." I lean back after taking a sip and search for something to talk about. Anything that'll get our minds off of tonight's events. "So it's crazy what Dr. Strider said about me, isn't it?"

"Yeah." She's still distracted, so I push on.

"Do you really think I could learn how to control it?"

She sets her wine glass down on the coffee table. "No offense, Ethan, but I don't really want to talk about Dr. Strider."

"Oh. Sorry." I take another sip.

Her heels are sitting on the chair adjacent to us. Her legs are tucked underneath her and she's leaning sideways on the back of the couch, facing me.

"It's just been a weird night," she says.

"Definitely. You feeling any better?"

She shrugs. "I guess so. Thanks for being there for me. I don't know if I would've kept it together without you."

"I wouldn't have either."

We hold each other's gaze for a moment and then she says, "We should go to bed."

Silently, we go through the motions of our nightly routine. It feels strangely foreign after tonight's events. I've slept over at

Chapter Five

Emma's enough for it not to be weird. This is just . . . discontent.

Finally, we lay down in bed. I wrap my arms around her and she clicks off the light. A moment later, I feel her pulling at my arm and tightening our embrace.

As we try to drift off to sleep, I hold her tight as she cries.

———

THE FOLLOWING MONDAY is my first day back at Wyatt. Already I'm exhausted from this weekend.

Luckily, it's not a hard workday since there's a small "Welcome Back!" party on my floor. I know Emma is the one behind it. I'm not close with a lot of my coworkers. Sure, we work together to get the numbers for our floors up, but other than the group "Get Well Soon" card, I wasn't expecting much of a reaction from my return. Our jobs are so isolated that we don't have to collaborate on projects. We all just clock in and out. It's just a job.

Balloons pinned at my cubicle read "Welcome Back!" as does the cake in the break room. After the initial rush of greetings this morning, the office returns to its normal pace until lunchtime when we all gather in the break room to have cake.

It's funny. There are fifty people on my floor and I only know maybe half of them. But after my stint in the hospital, everyone knows me. Lots of cards, well wishes, and smiling faces. It's nice, but I don't know how much of it is motivated by Emma.

After I cut the cake, everyone breaks off into their own social groups, leaving me and Emma to ourselves. The crowd begins to clear out and return to work within half an hour. Emma and I are the only ones left to clean up.

"This was nice, Emma. Thanks."

She waves her hand at me. "Everyone missed you while you were gone. We're just happy to see you back."

I smile, because we both know she missed me the most. Even though she'd deny it.

"I'm sure your brother is probably glad to get you out of the apartment," she says, stacking paper plates with cake remnants on them.

FUSE: ORIGIN

"With all my trips to the clinic, I actually haven't been home that much." I take the stack from her and deposit them into the trash. "Plus, he's been taking on as many stories as possible."

"What did he say about all this clinic business?"

I hold open the garbage bag for her. "Haven't told him much."

"Why not?"

"It's stupid. He's just going to make fun of me for it." I shrug. "Besides, I'm not even sure I believe Dr. Strider's theory."

"You shot lightning out of your fingertips. I've seen it. I'd say his theory is pretty believable."

I roll my eyes. "I doubt that it's permanent."

"I'm just saying, be careful plugging things in," she counters. "It's hard to stay away from electricity when you work for an energy company."

"Whatever," I say to end the conversation. "How's your new job going?"

"All right, I guess. I mean, it's so much better than walking through the steps of 'Control, Alt, Delete' with Agnes from the fourth floor. The pay's nice too. It's just . . . so much political stuff up there."

"Really? Just one floor up? Wow, you've reached your peak. It's only downhill from here." I whistle as I drop my hand down, making muffled explosion sounds.

She smiles and continues. "But as your boss, I get to commission fun stuff like this party. Pretty cool, huh?"

"Oh, it was a real rager. Not sure I can get back to work now, I'm so wound up."

She laughs. "Shut up."

"Hey, do you mind if I skip out of here, like, half an hour early?"

She lifts her eyebrows. "Already cutting your hours on your first day back?"

"Funny. No, I'm supposed to have dinner with Cale and Myra."

"I suppose that's fine. As long as I get you tomorrow. I still owe you a dinner."

I'm beaming, but I don't care who sees me. "You're the best,

Chapter Five

thank you." I kiss her on the cheek and turn to head back to work, but she calls for me.

"Ethan?"

"Yeah?"

"Um . . . Friday—"

"Was scary. I'm just glad neither of us were alone. You really helped me keep it together."

She blushes. "Right. Thanks, though."

"Anytime."

———

I'M SURPRISED TO see Myra is already working in the kitchen when I get home. She's standing at the sink, rinsing off potatoes.

"Hey," she says. Her curly hair is pinned up in a bun. A few strands of curls have fallen out and bounce as she turns her head. "How was your first day back?"

"Good. They had a party for me at lunch, which was pretty cool."

She beams. "How nice!"

"Yeah, it was a surprise." I rap my fingers against the island counter. "Where's Cale? I thought he was making dinner?"

She shakes her head and swats her hand in the air. "Oh, you know. Producing his segment last minute before the news tonight. He just called and said he's on his way."

I nod. "Good, yeah. I'm going to change real quick. I'll be right back."

By the time I emerge from my room in a fresh set of clothes, Cale is home. He's perched on the barstool by the island and telling Myra about his day.

" . . . the police are suspecting the Martelli family."

"What are you guys talking about?" I take a seat next to him.

"There was a drive-by shooting Friday night in Hopman. A few blocks away from the Wyatt plant. Did you hear anything when you came home from your interview?"

"Oh . . . yeah. Emma and I were there."

"You were *there*?" Myra blurts. She's mixing something on

the stove but she turns and looks at me, wooden spoon in the air.

"Are you all right? Why didn't you tell me?" Cale asks.

"We're fine. After they shot the guy, they just kind of drove off." I try to downplay it. Cale and Myra don't need to be worried about me. I've promised myself that I'll be more careful when I go down to the clinic from now on. Daylight only, take a cab if possible.

"Ethan, you saw someone get shot!" Myra exclaims. "It's okay if you need to talk about it."

"Guys, relax. I'm fine. I didn't actually see anything. I was too busy ducking for cover to pay attention." I just want it to go away. To stop talking about it.

"What happened? Did anyone see you?" Cale pushes.

"I think the driver might have." I point to Myra. "Do you need a hand?"

She cocks an eyebrow at me. "Did you call the police?"

I sigh and give in to the fact that I'm now elbow-deep in the interrogation. "I didn't have to. They were already on their way."

"If this *is* the Martelli family, then you and Emma need to be extra careful," Myra warns. "We've been working with the OPD at the office on this. Organized crime has been taking over parts of the city, and the police haven't been able to stop them. There are too many people involved. When they think they've found a ringleader, it turns out there are a whole layer of others. The police are working on getting their men in the Martelli's circles, but that takes time."

The extensiveness of the crime family in Olympia is surprising to me. I knew they existed fifty years ago, but I thought they were mostly dormant now. Like a retirees' social club.

"So what you're saying is that Emma and I are both risking our lives every time we step outside?"

"That's *exactly* what she's saying, Ethan!" Cale stands and fishes in his pocket for his phone. "I think I have an old friend who works at the station—"

"He does," I interrupt. "Tucker says hi."

"That's good. Tucker's good." He seems to feel a little better.

"He said he might have an idea who it is."

CHAPTER FIVE

Cale shakes his head. "I'm not surprised."

"How many cops are working on this?" I ask Myra. "I haven't heard much about this family."

"The cops are undercover," Cale says. "They would be sitting ducks for the Martellis if they drove around in their police cars and uniforms. And they can't tell the media because obviously that'd take out any surprise."

Myra nods. "It's true. It takes time to gain the family's trust. Especially if you're not Italian." Her position at city hall is probably the only reason Cale, a member of the media, knows about them.

"So what am I supposed to do? Spend my life looking over my shoulder?"

Cale shrugs. "It sucks, but there's nothing more you can do. What's done is done. Hopefully it'll get better. Damn well better not get worse. First the coma, now the mafia. Don't tell Mom."

I can't believe what I'm hearing. I don't want to be afraid of going anywhere by myself. I don't want to have to stick to crowds and public places in order to ensure my safety. I'm already considering calling Emma, telling her to stay safe and let her know what's going on. Luckily, we work downtown. Most of my commute is within a crowd.

I look up at Cale with wide eyes. "Emma is the IT manager at Wyatt. She goes down to the plant frequently for meetings. She went down by herself Friday."

"I'm giving you Tucker's number. Call him and tell him that you know about the Martelli family. Then call Emma and tell her not to go anywhere alone."

I think of how terrified she was that night. If she knows it's not over, she'll worry herself sick. I look up at them again and ask, "We could just be overreacting, right? I mean, maybe it wasn't the Martellis?"

Myra looks at Cale and then me. "Be careful, Ethan."

Chapter Six

"Wait a minute," Emma says, waving her wine glass at me. We're sitting on the couch at her apartment. "You're saying that because we just happened to be walking by when the shooting happened that we're the next ones on the hit list?"

"We could be," I say. When I called to tell her what Cale and Myra told me, she wanted me to come over. After our awkward conversation at lunch, I figured it was better to tell her in person anyway. "I talked to Tucker earlier, and he said that as long as we stay out of Hopman, we should be safe. It sounds like the Martellis are more focused on that district."

"I have to go down there! I have another meeting at the plant tomorrow afternoon!" She stares blankly at the floor and brings her glass to her mouth but doesn't drink.

"I'm sorry. I wish I could take you myself, but I have a PT appointment."

She lets out a deep breath. "Yeah. I just wish we weren't there that night, you know?" She rubs her forehead. "This is a nightmare."

"Hey, relax. This will hopefully blow over in a couple weeks.

Chapter Six

They'll find someone more important to mess with. We'll be off the hook."

Her head pops up. "This is the mob, Ethan. We'll never be off the hook!"

I let the weight of her words sink in. We saw one shooting. I don't even know the guy we saw. Why would they want to kill us? If this really is a big crime family, then surely they have more important things to take care of.

At least, that's what I'm trying to convince myself of. I'm still scared to go to sleep tonight. The dreams last night were horrible. And now that I know we could be a target, the dreams are likely to get worse.

After we finish our glasses of wine, I put in a new deadbolt on her door. The landlord isn't going to be happy we put it in without permission, but at least Emma will feel safer.

I suggest watching TV, but even though we watch a couple of our shows on Netflix, I can tell neither of us is really paying attention. After a while, I see the clock reads 10:34.

"I should go. The boss is going to expect me to be well rested tomorrow." I stand and reach toward the ceiling, my back popping and cracking.

"Damn straight!" She forces a smile and walks me to the door.

"Are you going to be okay by yourself tonight?" I pull her closer to me. "I can stay if you want."

She kisses me. "I'll be fine, dear. I'm going to have to get over it eventually."

"I'm not going to think less of you if—"

She puts her hand on my lips. "Ethan, I'll be fine. See you tomorrow. You still coming for dinner?"

"I'm going to stop at the clinic after work, but—"

"Please don't. That man got shot two blocks away from there. It's too dangerous."

"Don't worry. I'll be fine."

"I won't think any less of you—"

I laugh. "Okay! I get it." I kiss her again. "Seriously, though, I'll be okay."

She huffs. "Just be careful."

Fuse: Origin

WHEN I GET to work the next morning, I spot an envelope with my name written on it propped up against my monitor screen.

Probably another "Welcome back!" card. I think Susan was off yesterday and missed the party. It's probably from her.

I open it and my hands immediately begin to shake. It's a note, printed from a computer.

They're watching you is all it says.

Who sent this? Why? How long ago were they here? Did I pass them in the hallway? Are they watching me already?

Tucking the note back in the envelope, I rest my mouth against my fist and try to calm myself down. Think of what I can do to keep me and Emma safe.

I have to tell Tucker. If the police are going to find them, they have to know that these guys know about us.

"Staff meeting," Emma calls to the room. She sees me jump and points to me. "That means you, Pierce." Cracking a smile, she disappears into the conference room.

I can't tell Emma what I found. That'll only freak her out, and she won't be able to focus on anything else.

At lunch I'll call Tucker and tell him what's going on. Maybe once I have a better idea about where we go from here, I'll tell Emma about the note. In the meantime, though, I tuck it inside my top desk drawer, safely out of sight.

———

DEAN AND I are both happy with how far I've come at PT. Even after a long day at the office, I'm still doing so much better than I was the first day. Still, I tend to shock Dean every time I see him. That's a side effect of my lightning strike he can't fix.

Which is why I'm now in a cab heading toward the clinic. It's late, but I'm hoping Alex can answer a few more questions I have about my newfound ability. If Wes thinks I can control it, I want to learn how. The shooting helped put things into perspective for me. My body was changed from the strike, sure, and there's nothing I can do about that. What I can do is learn how to adjust. Especially if that note I got is true and the Martellis are watching me. I need to make sure Emma and I are protected.

It's times like these that make me wish I had a gun. The closest I have is my static shocks. If nothing else, talking to Alex and Wes will help me get my mind off those pictures and the attack for a little while.

The receptionist at the front desk at the clinic doesn't let me past the waiting room, so I sit in one of the metal chairs with the other patients. The clientele is varied. There's the homeless man who smells like he crawled out of a sewer, the elderly couple that probably have insurance issues, and the single mom with three kids that won't sit still. I'm the only one who isn't coughing, bleeding, or dying.

Finally the receptionist takes me back to an examination room where I wait another twenty minutes. I try explaining to her that I just need to speak with Alex, but she tells me to wait for the doctor.

I'm startled when I see Wes enter the room.

"Where's Al—Dr. Fletcher?"

"Night off," he says. "I wasn't expecting you to be my next patient."

"Yeah, well, I tried explaining to the lady at the front desk, but she wouldn't listen."

Wes nods. "So what brings you in, then?"

"You told me the other day that you think I'll be able to control my abilities," I start.

He nods. "That's right. With training."

"How?"

He's quiet a moment. The only sound is the tapping of his fingers on the counter. "Let me think about it a little while longer. There may be something I can come up with that'll help you focus your energy. Are you still shocking people?"

"All the time." I think of the rides on the subway when I accidentally bumped into someone and shocked them—the one time so much that I saw a visible spark. I'm waiting for the day I stop the whole train.

He nods. "Okay. Give me some time to come up with a few ideas."

"I don't want to have to take any pills." I don't want to think what would happen if I miss a day. Not to mention, I'm not even sure a drug exists that could stifle the charges running through my body without some serious side effects.

Wes shakes his head. "That's not what I'm thinking. I'll let you know as soon as I come up with something. In the meantime, go someplace where you'll be away from anything that could hurt you or anyone around you and try to release this energy. I know that's easier said than done, but you won't know how to control it until you learn how to trigger it."

I snort. With the Martellis keeping an eye on me, I don't know if there's anywhere in the city I could go that they wouldn't follow me.

We leave it at that. Not the concrete answers I was looking for, but definitely something to work on. I'm curious to see what Wes comes up with to help control these abilities. I can't imagine there's anything medically for him to do, but then again, he's the mutation specialist. Not me.

The cab service has a half hour wait when I call for a ride home so I decide to risk the subway. The sun hasn't quite set yet, so I figure I'm safe. It's only two blocks from the clinic anyway, and I'll go around the scene of the crime from last night. I'm not a total idiot.

Halfway there, I'm knocked to the ground out of nowhere. Hard. I hit my head on the sidewalk and my scalp starts bleeding. I turn just as a fist comes down to my face.

"You got mighty big balls, kid, I'll give you that."

At first all I notice are his tan boots and frayed jeans. Just before he punches me again and I collapse on the ground.

My head is spinning and my face already begins to swell, but I swing my legs and trip the man to the ground. I force myself to get to my feet. Otherwise, I'd be a dead man. I take a few steps back, but my attacker is quick. He's a couple feet

Chapter Six

away and his gun is pointed right at me.

"Nothing personal, kid."

"Wait!" I shout, putting up my hands. White streaks of lighting erupt from my palms and collide with the man. His body spasms from the repeated blows. I'm horrified, but can't seem to stop it. Lightning just keeps coming and coming until I'm finally drained. Too exhausted to keep my head up or even stand. I slump to the ground as the man falls flat on his back.

After I catch my breath, I scramble over to him. His clothes are burned away and his skin is blackened at two spots on his chest where the shocks hit him. I place my fingers along his neck but don't feel a pulse. My hands begin to shake.

Did I really just kill this man? I didn't even touch him! I didn't even have his gun! What am I going to do now? I'm going to jail.

The events from the other night flash in my mind. That happened two blocks from here. In a matter of a few days, I've witnessed two murders in this neighborhood, one at my own hands.

With tears in my eyes I try to call 911, but my phone is fried. It's too hot to hold, and I drop it on the sidewalk, where it shatters. I look around for help, but the street has gone quiet.

In my head I replay the few words he said to me. He was probably a part of the Martelli family. Which means he might not have been acting alone. I look back and see the clinic is only half a block away. I make a run for it, crossing the vacant street and bursting inside.

"There's a man . . . " I start, but I'm too wiped from the run. I collapse on the floor. The receptionist behind the front desk runs to me. I hear her call for help, but my vision is gone.

I feel myself being lifted onto a stretcher and wheeled into a room as a commotion of voices wonder what happened. The noise suddenly ceases, and I realize I'm not in a room. I'm in an elevator. I don't remember there being an elevator in the building. Not even a minute later I've stopped moving, and I feel hands pulling my shirt open and placing plastic pieces on my chest. I'm reliving my week in the hospital all over again.

My vision begins to return, and I see that Wes is the one

working on me. I'm hooked up to a heart monitor that gives off a slow beat every other second. As I take a deep breath, the beats pick up speed, and I can see him breathe a sigh of relief.

"Mr. Pierce, can you hear me?"

I try to speak, but my throat is so dry. He grabs my arm and sticks in an IV.

I look around and try to figure out where I am. Steel beams run along the ceiling, supporting the floor above. Curtain walls box me in and prevent me from seeing the rest of the room.

After a few more minutes, I'm finally able to ask, "Where are we?"

"The basement of the clinic." He lifts a cup toward me, and I sip water from a straw. "Dr. Fletcher and I have been using this space as a laboratory of sorts to examine your condition. Until we understand this better, I think it's best if we keep this private. We don't want to be bombarded with questions."

I nod.

"What happened? Debbie said you mentioned a man before you passed out."

"He jumped me," I say, eyes closed. "I killed him. With my power. He's dead!" The temporary distraction from passing out having faded, my memories come back full force. With it, my emotions.

"Who? Where did his happen?"

I try to swallow the lump in my throat but it's no use. A man is dead because of me. I'm a murderer. "Outside. He jumped me. He's dead," I repeat.

The sound of clicking heels precedes Alex into the room.

"What happened? Are you okay? There's a load of police cars on the street out front." The words fall out of her mouth all at once and her eyes scan over me and my bare chest.

"He was attacked," Wes tells her. "He, uh, *shocked* him."

I shake my head again. If I wasn't so dehydrated, tears would be rolling down my face. Instead I just shake.

Alex squeezes my free hand and looks at me with pity in her eyes. "Ethan, you couldn't help it. You can't control what's been happening to you."

Chapter Six

"But I should!" I snap. "*I* did this! *I* killed him!" A few minutes later, my eyes grow heavy until my body relaxes and I'm out. Wes probably slipped a sedative in my IV. I'm left to relive the memory of that man's body convulsing as the life slipped out of his eyes.

I deserve to be locked up.

———

WHEN I WAKE up, I'm upstairs in one of the examination rooms. Cale's sitting in the corner playing on his phone with his head resting on his other hand, and Myra leans on her knees and watches me.

"Hey," she says when she sees my eyes open. "How are you feeling?"

I shrug in response, still unsure whether I can talk. I don't want them to see me cry. They wouldn't understand. They would have to know what's been going on with me to understand, and that is too much to handle right now.

"You've had a rough couple of weeks." Cale stows his phone in his pocket. "You should stay away from places like this. I thought we discussed this."

Myra shoots him a look and reaches for my hand. "It's a good thing you were so close to the clinic when it happened."

I nod, unsure of how much they know. "Yeah. I'm lucky."

"Ethan, what's been going on with you?" Cale asks. "You've been acting strange the last couple weeks. Coming down here on a regular basis, getting involved with all these murders—"

Myra grabs his hand to silence him and adds, "We're just really worried about you."

On top of everything, I feel guilty now too. I've never lied to Cale before. Not about anything big, anyway. But if I did tell him about my ability, he either wouldn't believe me or he'd lock me up in a padded room to stay out of trouble.

"Good, you're awake," Tucker says when he steps through the door. He looks at my brother and smiles. "Cale, how've you been?" They shake hands, Cale introduces Myra, and they smile and make brief small talk. Meanwhile, I'm laid up in a makeshift hospital bed trying not to fall apart.

"Ethan," Tucker says, turning back to me. "Do you mind if I ask you a few questions?"

I toss up my hands. "Sure." It's not like I really have a choice.

"Start at the beginning. What happened?"

"I was walking to the subway when this guy came up behind me and pushed me to the ground. He pulled out a gun and . . ." I trail off, not sure whether to lie or tell the truth. Nobody would believe the truth, but what would be a convincing lie? "I don't know," I continue. "I think after the other day my subconscious is blocking it out."

That was a lame-ass excuse, Ethan. God, I'm stupid sometimes.

He studies me a moment and then asks, "What were you doing out this way again? I figured after what happened before, you'd steer clear of places like this."

"Visiting a friend. Dr. Fletcher is the one who treated me in the hospital."

"According to some of the people in the clinic, Dr. Fletcher wasn't here when you first showed up."

"Dr. Strider is a friend too." I sneak a look at Cale and Myra to see their reaction. They're both giving Tucker skeptical looks.

"You don't think Ethan did anything wrong, do you?" Cale asks with an edge to his voice.

"Well, I don't know about that. Any potential witnesses aren't talking. But you said he pulled a gun on you, and yet he's the one dead, without a single bullet wound." Tucker taps his pad of paper against his palm. "I'm not sure what to believe."

"If it wasn't a bullet wound, how *did* the man die?" Myra asks.

Tucker looks to Cale and then back to her. "The coroner is looking at him now."

"Whatever they find, I'm sure Ethan didn't do anything," Myra says.

"We'll just have to see what they find, then." Tucker turns back to me. "If you remember anything, give me a call."

Chapter Six

Cale turns on me once Tucker's out of earshot. "Ethan, you need to find another doctor. Hopman is too dangerous."

"I wanted to talk to Alex," I mutter. I feel about six inches tall. Cale has every right to be angry. To be worried. Coming down here was stupid, but I just can't deal with any of that right now. I just killed a man and I can't even fess up to it.

Myra shakes her head. "Ethan, what if you had died tonight?"

I shrug.

Cale rolls his eyes. "That's all you have to say?"

I glare at him, fighting back more tears. "I'll be fine."

"You shouldn't have to look over your shoulder every day," she argues.

"You didn't even go a week without getting your ass kicked," Cale adds.

"Are we done? I'm tired, and I'd really like to get home."

"You're not off the hook," Cale says.

"Ethan, I don't think you realize just how dangerous this area is," Myra argues. "This district alone contributes seventy percent of the whole city's crime rate. That's insane! You know that firsthand. And for whatever reason, there are no programs in place to combat the drugs, sex trafficking, and murders going on over here."

That got my attention.

"What about the Martellis?" They're the only connection I have with crime in the Hopman District. To me, it seems the Martellis operate only in Hopman, even though I know that's probably not true.

"They're mostly in Little Italy and Midtown. They have some operations in Hopman, like they do the rest of the city, but I don't believe they're the cause of everything."

"Doesn't your boss represent the Hopman District?" I ask. "What are you going to do about all this crime?"

"Ethan . . . " Cale warns.

Myra ignores him. "I don't know! Frank Lloyd doesn't seem to care that the rest of the council is on our asses about our cancer of a district. I've suggested parades, street festivals, police cameras, improved funding to the area libraries and schools, but the proposals never make it very far."

"Who votes them down?" Cale asks.

She shrugs. "Nobody, really. They just seem to lose momentum, and then it's months, sometimes even a year later, and the whole proposal is just gone. The city is on a rebound, that's for sure, but there isn't a lot of money to work with in the meantime. The solar roadways are great, but the construction costs put us way out of budget. And the city's even splitting some of the costs with Wyatt!"

"What about the history of the neighborhood?" I ask.

"Maybe that could be your angle," Cale adds. "Didn't Manhattan Avenue extend all the way down to the waterfront?"

"Yeah, this was primarily a black neighborhood that started spilling over into the city's elite university district. No wonder they put the expressway right through the neighborhood. But nobody's going to admit to that." She shakes her head. "I don't know. There's still a lot of original buildings. Maybe there's something there. Historic tax breaks through the state or something. In the meantime, though, you need to stay away from here, Ethan."

I've never really walked through the heart of the Hopman neighborhood, only the outskirts. If what I've seen on the fringes is only a glimpse of what goes on in the center of the neighborhood, I don't think a street party and some tax breaks are going to turn the area around anytime soon.

CHAPTER SEVEN

On the subway, I stare blankly as images from yesterday keep flashing in my mind. The determination on the man's face. The swing of his fist just before it collided with my cheek. The terror that we both felt as the power surged out of my body, striking him. Killing him.

I still ache from it all, but I deserve it. Deserve worse. He's dead and I'm responsible. Even though he's the one who attacked me first, he didn't need to die. Especially not like that.

My reflection in the window contrasts the way I feel inside. The other riders probably think I just have a hangover or had a long day at work. They don't know that they're in the midst of a murderer. Can I go on pretending that I'm not?

And yet I have a feeling that attack was just the first attempt by the Martelli family to find me. I need to be prepared for more attacks. I can imagine the way criminals and the like look at me. I'm thin, nerdy, an easy target. Hell, even when I used to wrestle with my brother as a kid I would always scream uncle just to get him to stop. There was no competition.

I arrive at my next therapy appointment early. Dean's not

here yet, but I start without him. Instead of my usual walk on the treadmill, I try a slow jog, clicking up the speed after a few minutes until I'm in an all-out run.

"What the hell do you think you're doing?" Dean barks. He comes over and hits the "Stop" button on the machine. "Are you trying to give yourself a heart attack?"

The receptionist and the other therapist glance into the room and my face goes red. I've never seen Dean angry before. It's almost terrifying. As if I need another reason to be scared.

My chest heaves as I try to steady my breath. He's right. I'm not at that level yet. At the rate I'm going, I never will be.

"What would've happened if I came in here and saw you passed out on the floor?" Dean berates me, shouting loudly enough for them to hear out on the street. He waves his hand between the machine and me. "How long until someone revived you? What if you didn't survive? Don't do that to your family or your friends." He turns and makes a fist to calm himself.

"I wasn't going that fast," I mutter.

He whirls around. "Doesn't matter. Too fast for you." A vein in his neck twitches. "You survived a fucking lightning strike. Give yourself a break!"

I let out a big breath of air. Definitely not in the mood for a lecture. Especially as I watch other people purposefully pass by the open door to get a peek at the yelling.

"Maybe I'll just go home." I hop off the treadmill and gather my things.

"Maybe you should." He puts his hands on hips and watches as I walk out.

Humiliating.

Here I am, trying to be something I'm not. I wasn't thinking about anything else other than the fact that I can't kill another man. Not again. I narrowly escaped arrest yesterday—may even still get charged. I can't lose control like that. For all I know he was just going to kick me around to figure out what I saw and scare me from talking to the cops. Too late for that. I never want to find myself in a situation like that again.

But what did I expect to happen from suddenly trying to

Chapter Seven

run a marathon? I haven't stepped foot inside a gym since high school. I just wanted to become stronger, faster. I know I still need to, but I guess I'm not ready yet. Not according to Dean, anyway.

I NEED TO cool down after being yelled at like a little kid. Part of me wants to run outside just to prove to Dean that he can't control me. But deep down I know he's right. I would probably hurt myself.

Instead, I wander around downtown, meandering along West Division Street down to the Main Street Park right outside city hall. I take a seat near the fountain that marks the spot where the city's founder's house once stood and watch the water trickle into the basin.

When did this become my life? I'm running wild, scared of what's going to happen to me solely because I was in the wrong place at the wrong time.

My thoughts are interrupted by a phone call.

"Hey, Ethan, it's Tucker Cross." He sounds defeated.

"Hey, what's up?"

He lets out a sigh. "Well, this isn't easy, but I was wondering if you have a minute to come down to the station to answer some questions about the murders you witnessed."

All the air in my lungs seems to have vanished. "Oh. Uh, sure. Now?"

"Yeah, if you're free now."

I nod. "Yeah, I'm not too far. I'll be there in five minutes."

"Okay, great."

The call ends and I stare at the phone. More questions? That can't be good. Unless they just want to get my official statement.

A text pops up from Cale: *Where are you? When are you coming home?*

Annoyed that my every move is being watched, I reply: *Downtown. Not sure when I'll be home.*

I get it, they're all worried about me. But hovering over me isn't going to protect me from the people who are targeting me. Yesterday's attack proved that. Of course, wandering around on my own isn't helping things, either.

The police station is only two blocks north, so it doesn't take me long to get there. I wait by the receptionist's desk until Tucker comes to get me.

"Hey, Ethan." He's very serious now. "Thanks for coming in." He offers his hand and again I zap it.

"Yeah, no problem. What's up?"

He leads me to an interrogation room and takes a seat at the table.

My mouth has gone dry. I pull out the opposite chair and take a seat.

He motions to the mirror behind him. "There's no one back there."

I look up at it and nod, swallowing the lump in my throat. A whole new kind of fear runs through me.

"It's just a quiet place for us to talk."

I nod again, not sure if I can trust my voice.

"Okay," he says with a breath of air. "The coroner said the cause of death for Dominic Lacey was electrocution." He slides a photo and the coroner report across the table to me. It's the man I killed. "Nobody can figure out how it happened." He studies me a bit and then asks, "You didn't see any loose power lines or anything, did you? Maybe a taser?"

I shake my head. "No, not that I could see."

He tucks away the papers and lets out another sigh. "I'm going to be honest with you. The rest of the men on this case consider you a person of interest."

I gulp and try to stay calm.

"You witnessed two murders within a week, both in Hopman, not far from each other. These are facts. Undisputed. You were there. People saw you. You admitted to your whereabouts as well."

This is it. He's going to arrest me. They'll find some motive for me and put me on trial. I'm going to prison.

Tucker holds up a finger and continues. "Now there's also

the fact that you weren't responsible for the death of Carlos Wilson—the homeless man whose death started all this for you."

I shake my head. "No. I didn't even know him."

"And based off the drawing the sketch artist came up with after talking to you and Emma, we believe the driver to be involved with the Martellis."

Not at all surprised by that.

"After you witnessed that shooting, you received the note at work indicating that you were being followed, possibly even threatened. Later that day, you were attacked. The issue here is, no one saw that particular altercation."

"So what does that mean?" I don't want to lie. I killed that man. I didn't know him. Didn't even know his name until two minutes ago. He was a stranger. A messenger. In a way, I'm no better than the men who killed Carlos Wilson.

"Well, Dr. Wesley Strider says you weren't carrying anything that could generate enough electricity to kill someone the day you ran into Mr. Lacey. I saw you myself afterward, and I can vouch for the fact that no weapon of that kind was at the scene." He shrugs. "If you ask me, you didn't do it. Yet again, you were the victim."

With all my might, I fight to keep emotion from my face.

"So what I need from you is a confirmation that you weren't carrying a weapon on you that day and that you had no intent to harm Mr. Lacey."

I shake my head. "No. No weapon, and I didn't want to kill him. I didn't even know him."

He nods and stands. "All right. That's all I need."

"That's it?" A weight lifts from my shoulders as I get to my feet.

"Easy enough, right? I'll walk you out." He leads me back out to the front entrance and, to my surprise, follows me down the sidewalk a bit.

Once we're a good distance away from the station, he grips my shoulder and says, "Another detective might drag this out longer. Look into your phone records, internet history, bank statements, whatever." He rubs his chin. "I'll say this, off the record: I think you're just being targeted. The second attack, the note at your office—they all point to you being the victim."

He looks down the street at the cars whizzing by. The sun has set, but the streetlights make the area glow.

"Be careful, Ethan. These guys aren't going to stop until they get what they want. Stick to crowds, stay in well-lit areas, and always tell someone where you're going. This will go away, but you need to be careful."

I nod. "Thank you. For everything."

He shakes my hand again, apparently ignoring the zap I give him. "I hope I didn't scare you too bad in there. There are just some motions I have to go through to do my due diligence. Now get home and stay safe."

Bidding him good-bye, I head back toward Main Street, lost in thought. My nerves are completely shot now. I can feel how tight my back and shoulders are. Worse, the zaps between my fingers seem to be constant now.

Hooking around to Ellsworth Avenue to avoid the police station and potentially running into Tucker again, I head up to the next subway station to take the train to Emerson Bluffs. The lakefront park at the north end of the city is the only place I can think of to expend the energy building up in me, like Wes suggested. With the growing darkness, it's the perfect cover.

I get off the subway at Emerson Bluffs and follow the dimly-lit path into the park. I've been here a million times. The park is huge, but so is the edge of the cliff down to the lake. In the daylight, there are so many great vantage points to the beach below and the city's skyline. It's a popular wedding location.

It's at Bridal Point that I finally take my hands out of my pockets and hold them out toward the water. With a deep breath, I try to summon the energy and let it flow through me.

It doesn't take long before white lightning streaks from my hands out toward the water, arcing in the air, lighting up the rocky cliffs below.

After just a few minutes, I feel myself weaken. Now I start to worry about being jumped. Even without the lightning, I'm too weak to defend myself. So I forgo Dean's warnings and jog down

Chapter Seven

the path and out of the park, not stopping until I'm back under the safety of a streetlight. My heart rate doesn't slow until I'm walking out of the subway stop by my apartment, happy that my fingers have stopped buzzing. Happy to finally be home.

CHAPTER EIGHT

It's amazing how environment can alter your perspective on things. I've been a little nervous about this meeting since Mr. Gotti asked me to visit Mr. Rizzoli at Tranidek last week. But so much has happened since then that I almost forgot about it.

My blasé attitude toward the meeting fades away as soon as I step inside the Midtown glass-faced high-rise. My office building has an antique charm to it, but Tranidek's building looks top-of-the-line. With the exception of their campus in Ashland, all of their operations are out of this tower, whereas Wyatt owns several properties.

Fighting through the crowd on their way out of the office, I ask the doorman which floor Frank Rizzoli's office is on.

"Mr. Rizzoli?" the man asks suspiciously.

I nod. "Yeah, I have a meeting with him at six."

Glancing at the clock, I see it's ten minutes to six.

"Just a moment." The doorman dials a number on a phone behind the counter. Likely verifying the accuracy of my story. My bruised face doesn't lend itself to an executive meeting. Since Tuesday's punch in the face, my skin has turned a very

Chapter Eight

unphotogenic black and blue. Luckily, my teeth are all still there and none of the blood vessels in my eyes popped. The cut on my scalp from where I hit the pavement is covered by my hair, although my head still throbs a bit.

After he gets off the phone, he smiles brightly and leads me around the corner to an elevator all on its own.

"This will take you right up to the 72nd floor. Mr. Rizzoli's office will be on the right."

"Thanks," I mutter and step into the elevator. His office is on the 72nd floor? That's gotta be close to the top.

My ears pop on the ride up, which is less than a minute long. The first thing I notice when I step out is the view of downtown along the edge of the lake. Wyatt Industries' administration building seems so tiny from this vantage point.

Pulling myself away from the window, I turn toward the glass door and step through, telling the brunette woman at the front desk that I have an appointment. She leaves to tell Mr. Rizzoli, and I take a look around. The square footage for this floor seems to be a lot smaller than the ground level, but then, the building does come to a point at the top. I know because I can see it from my apartment. I checked.

There are two offices off this main one—likely for Mr. Rizzoli and Mr. Gotti. I wonder if the only ones working on this floor are those two and the secretary.

The brunette comes back out with a silver-haired man right behind her. He's wearing a blue suit with a red tie. A pair of black, thick-rimmed glasses sit inside his pocket.

"Mr. Pierce, so nice to finally meet you," he says. "Frank Rizzoli."

I smile and shake his hand, hoping he doesn't notice the shock that he's likely to feel, but he doesn't seem to flinch. Must be that my trip to Emerson Bluffs worked like Wes thought it would.

"Nice to meet you too."

He motions to his office and puts his hand on my back. "Come on in and we can chat."

The only walls that are solid are the ones facing the interior.

65

Fuse: Origin

The other two are glass from floor to ceiling, offering beautiful views of nearby Midtown buildings and the Olympia metro area.

He motions to the sitting area with two black leather arm-chairs near the corner windows. "Have a seat."

It's warm for October, but the changing leaves add a certain aesthetic to the view. The high-rises downtown give way to the trees in Chester Park. Even Olympia University's campus looks like a park with the colored leaves between the old buildings. Together, it balances out the scars of the city.

"Gorgeous, isn't it?" He takes the seat across from me.

"Uh, yeah." I sit up straighter and take it in. I feel like I should be on my best behavior for the man who's paying my medical bills. I can thank my clumsy hands on that plug for ever meeting him.

"You're the talk of the town these days."

"I wouldn't say that."

He offers a smirk. "Modest. I admire that. But it takes a strong man to be able to endure what you've gone through. Joe tells me you are already back to work at Wyatt."

I nod. "Yes sir." Sir? Yup, definitely nervous.

"You've got a great work ethic. Most folks your age are always looking for the easy way out."

"I don't think this city would allow anyone to take the easy way out."

He's quiet for a moment, and then he points toward the Wind Tunnel cutting through the city.

"Being that you work at Wyatt, I'm sure you're well aware of the solar roadways they're installing throughout the city."

"Yes sir, I think it's a great way to go green and create jobs." Why do I keep saying "sir"?

He smiles. "It's expensive, though."

"I'm sure it is."

"You know, Tranidek was the one to initiate the solar road-way concept."

"Uh, yeah. I heard that." Where's he going with this?

"After we lost my good friend Robert Moyer, Tranidek went through a rough spot. We were without a CEO to further

Chapter Eight

coordinate projects, and the city decided to bid out our idea to other companies, which is when Wyatt stepped in. They were officially chosen for the project a month after I was promoted from Robert's assistant to CEO."

I nod. I've heard this before—during my first job interview with Wyatt, actually, but they painted a different picture of Tranidek and its future. Back then, they didn't think that Tranidek would even be around today.

"What do you do at Wyatt now, Mr. Pierce?"

"IT tech support. Mostly just taking calls from people within the company, although I've filled in for customer support before, too."

He looks out the window again. "As I'm sure you've read in my letter, I did a little research on you when you started making headlines."

I lick my dry lips. "Oh yeah?"

He grins. "Nothing bad, I promise. No, I was quite impressed with your academic background. Actually, I'm surprised that after three years Wyatt hasn't utilized some of your development skills a bit more. I think it was your junior year at Olympia University that you developed several apps?"

Wow, he really did look into my history. Besides an article in the school paper and an A in my class, I didn't think a lot of people knew about it. Wyatt didn't seem to be that impressed by it. OU has a lot of tech majors, and Wyatt scooped up a lot of them when they hired me after they won the bid for the solar roadways.

"Yeah, I did a couple of them."

"Very impressive."

"Thanks."

He's quiet, and I steal another look out the window, watching as cars pile up on the highways snaking through the city.

"Since I took Mr. Moyer's job, I've been working on building up the reputation of the company, back to where it was before we lost the roadway bid."

I nod.

"It's unlikely that we'll get the bid back for the whole project, but I may be able to negotiate a deal that would split the project in half."

"But Wyatt's installing the solar roadways."

"For now, but I have reason to believe that they're having financial difficulties. This is quite an expensive project, as I've said."

"What makes you think they're having trouble?"

"Stock market projections, mostly. Customers have been complaining of power outages during construction. It's getting colder, nobody wants to lose their heat. Not to mention, having their competitor take care of their own employee better than them didn't help matters."

I want to ask why he paid my bills at all, but I'm more interested to see where he's going with the point he's trying to make.

"Tranidek is working on developing software that's superior to Wyatt's. I want our customers to be able to track where outages are in the grid, whether someone is responding to those outages, and when they can expect to have them fixed. The software will also be able to warn customers of changes in roadway patterns and other street closures while this new technology is rolled out."

"That sounds very cool."

"If you're at all interested, I would like to offer you a position here at Tranidek. Not in IT tech support, but where you actually belong: development."

I stare at him blankly, not full comprehending what he just said. "Is this what you were referring to in your letter?"

He smiles widely now, flashing his bright white teeth. "Yes, Mr. Pierce. I would love to have you on board at Tranidek. We definitely could use your expertise with the rest of our team. You'd jump right in, and you'd be compensated well, I promise you that. Whatever you're making at Wyatt, we'll pay you more."

I struggle for words. I figured the position he was talking about in his letter was the same thing I'm doing at Wyatt. Some people work for years and still end up only designing websites in a basement office. How did I jump from working in a call center to being offered a development job at a major company?

Chapter Eight

"Sleep on it. This is a big decision."

"Okay," I mutter. "Um . . . thank you. This is unexpected."

"I know. I wanted to make the offer personally to show you just how serious I am. But please, don't mention this to anyone at Wyatt. Not until you've made a decision, at least. I've been told we've already had a few calls from some of their people. Make this decision for yourself."

I nod. "Yeah, of course."

"I'd also like to invite you to a dinner party this weekend at my condo. Just me and a couple colleagues and their wives. You can bring a friend if you'd like."

I try not to show my surprise at the invitation. "Oh wow. Thank you! That'd be great."

"I'll have Joe send the details. Maybe you'll have made a decision by then."

"Thank you! Yes, I'll be there."

He stands and shakes my hand again. "Mr. Pierce, I look forward to a successful working relationship." He walks me to the elevator. "Have a good night."

When the elevator doors close, leaving me alone in the box, I finally let myself relax, and a big smile spreads across my face.

Wow. I wonder when I'll wake up from this dream. But my sore eye when I smile reminds me that this is reality. Wyatt may be the biggest company in Olympia right now, but if Tranidek is going to pay me more... There's so much to consider. I've only been back at Wyatt for a few days.

The dinner party makes me nervous, though. It will be nice, sure, but I'm not exactly used to rubbing elbows with people like Frank Rizzoli. Especially when I'm an ant compared to the rest of them. I'm sure not everyone there will share the same sentiment as Mr. Rizzoli about my potential at Tranidek.

When I get out onto the street, I pull out my phone and call Emma as I turn down a side street, away from the hustle and bustle of Caulkins Street.

I hear the ringing stop, but she doesn't say anything. Pulling the phone away from my ear for a moment, I see the call hasn't been disconnected.

Fuse: Origin

"Hello? Emma?"

"Is this your girl?" a husky man's voice asks.

I stop in the middle of the sidewalk, my heart pumping faster than it did this morning on the treadmill. "Where is she?"

"She was good. A bit of a screamer." A voice chuckles in the background.

"Let her go," I say, knowing my words mean nothing to them. "Where is she?"

The line goes dead, and I fight everything that's bubbling up inside me. I don't know whether I want to throw up, cry, run, or collapse on the ground. My world is shaken and I don't know what to do.

CHAPTER NINE

Inquisitive eyes watch me as I run through the front doors of the clinic. There are only two people in the waiting room, both of whom seem perfectly healthy. Likely waiting for other people to finish up with Alex or one of her colleagues.

I'm not here to see them, though. I just need to use the computer in the basement. I need somewhere to go where I can be sure I'm safe.

Ironically, that safe spot is in Hopman, the very district I suspect they have Emma.

On my way over here, I called 911. They wanted more information than I had. Despite telling me to stay on the line, I couldn't just sit there and have them continue to tell me to stay calm and get to safety. Not while Emma is being . . . God, what the hell are they doing to her?

The computer in the basement is slow to boot up, but once it's running, it works well enough for me. My college pastime of hacking is perfect for this. In a matter of minutes, I'm logged into the grid, the city's electrical network that runs through the streets of Olympia thanks to Wyatt Industries' solar roadways.

Fuse: Origin

The new technology is hooked up to every electrical device in the city's network. With it, I can track which cell tower the call from the thug connected with and trace it back to Emma's location.

Hopefully she's still there.

"Ethan?" Wes comes to stand over my shoulder and watches my fingers fly over the keyboard, punching in code like second nature. "What's going on? What are you doing?"

"They have Emma."

"Who's Emma? What are you talking about?"

"They answered the phone when I tried to call her." My eyes don't leave the screen as I respond. "They have her somewhere. I'm just trying to—there! Otis and Adams Streets. That's nearby."

"What the hell, Ethan!" Alex storms down the steps, her heels clanging loudly on the metal staircase. "You can't just waltz in here like that! You had my patients freaking out!"

I stand and bypass her on my way to the stairs. "I gotta go help her."

"Ethan, think about it." Wes grabs my arm. "What are you going to do once you're there?"

I stop. I don't know what I'm going to do. I don't know the neighborhood, I don't know how to get into the building, I don't even know what I'm going to find once I'm there. And what if the police beat me there? I've already met with Tucker more times than I'd like. I don't want to add any more suspicion to my name.

But this is Emma. I can't just sit here and hope everything works out.

"Is someone going to tell me what's going on?" Alex demands.

"His friend Emma has been captured," Wes explains.

Alex's face drops in surprise. "Oh, Ethan, I'm so sorry."

"I don't know what I'm going to do." My voice betrays me. I've never been this angry before, but I'm also terrified.

She comes over and rubs my back. "You've called 911, right?"

I throw up and my hands and she backs away. "Of *course* I've called 911!"

"Then we need to let them take it from here," she says.

Chapter Nine

I shake my head in response.

"I may have something that could help." Wes walks over to one of the tall cabinets against the wall. Inside are several stacks of clothing. From what I can see, they're hospital gowns, lab coats, scrubs. Basic medical attire.

He pulls something black out and presses it between his palms. "Now, this is still a prototype."

"What is it?" I ask.

"Last week we were talking about how you should be able to learn to control your abilities. Your hyperenergy prior to release, your fatigue after you expel that energy. This suit will help you regulate all of that."

"Is this what you've been staying late to work on?" Alex feels the material.

He nods. "I thought it'd be helpful, at least for now, to create an equilibrium state for Ethan. The suit is lined with electrodes that will collect the charges your body generates, giving you less moments of hyperenergy and more control over when your power is executed."

"So I'm supposed to wear this all the time?" I approach him and hold up the suit. It's all black, with a single white lightning bolt stretching from the heart all the way down the right arm. The same arm my scar is on.

"I thought the lightning bolt would be a nice touch." He offers a quick grin. "You can wear it all the time if you'd like, but it's not necessary. In fact, I believe only a few hours a day will help you regulate your energy. The catch is, it's not a battery. The suit cannot hold any of the electricity you generate."

"So he's going to have to release the energy before he takes off the suit?" Alex asks.

Wes nods. "I wanted to implement the electrodes with fabric that would be comfortable to wear all day. It's a unique piece of clothing, but at the end of the day, it's still just a piece of clothing."

I study the suit for a moment, calculating my next move. It could help keep my location hidden in the dark. Perfect, since it's nighttime. I just need to find something to cover my face.

Fuse: Origin

"This will help me control my powers?"

Wes nods. "I believe so, yes. But be careful. It's still just a prototype. I'm sure there will be kinks to work out."

Alex looks from Wes to me and back. "You two aren't thinking of chasing after Emma's attackers, are you?"

I nod and Wes shrugs.

"You're both insane! I'm calling the cops."

"The boy's going to do whatever he wants anyway, Alex. It's best to send him off with as much preparation as possible." Wes argues.

"I'm not sending a patient on a suicide mission."

"What would you do?" I ask her. "What if it was your best friend? Your sister, mother, niece, whoever. I'm not—" I take a deep, shuddering breath. "I have a chance to help. I have to take it."

She lets out a sigh and closes her eyes. "Fine. But you're going to bring up the grid's traffic cameras so we can watch you."

"They're only at major intersections," Wes explains. "We won't be able to see much. And that's assuming none of them have been tampered with."

Shooting daggers at him with her eyes, she says, "I need it for my sanity."

"We've gotta move quick." I plop back in the chair and punch in the proper code to bring up the traffic cameras.

"I'll be right back," Wes says. "I need to run upstairs for something."

Alex and I nod, but both of us are focused on the computer screen.

After searching through the list of all of the traffic cameras in the city, I locate the correct district and then the closest corner. "That's the best I can do."

"Here, I found you these," Wes says when he returns. He hands me a black ski mask and a pair of black gloves. "Found them in my car. They're not much, but they'll work for tonight."

"There won't be another night," Alex says from beside me at the computer. She's studying the grainy picture as images flicker across it slowly.

Chapter Nine

I take the mask from Wes. "Thanks."

As Alex studies the traffic cams and Wes determines the best route for me using Google Maps, I escape behind the privacy curtain closing in the lone hospital bed down here. The same one I was laying in not that long ago.

Stripping down, I step into the suit and pull the zipper up in the back. It's snug against my body, but that gives me mobility. It reminds me of the clothes I wear to physical therapy, only tighter. The suit legs end at my ankles, and there's nothing else for me to wear on my feet other than my sneakers.

"Be careful with those," Wes warns when I step out from behind the curtain. "Everyone knows your connection to Emma. If they find a footprint anywhere that could lead back to you, this could all end disastrously."

My mind is going crazy trying not to think of the things they could be doing to her. It's already a disaster.

I kneel down to tie the laces tighter. Alex looks on disapprovingly.

"You know, if they find you there, *we* could get arrested too," she warns.

Wes ignores her. "I'll have to fashion you better footwear as well."

Just as I'm about to pull on the ski mask, my phone rings from the pocket of my pants where I left them behind the hospital curtain. It's Cale.

"Ethan, are you with Emma?"

My blood runs cold.

"Uh, no. Why?"

"Call her and make sure she's okay. I heard on the police scanner about an hour ago that there was a 911 call about a woman being kidnapped. With everything you guys have been involved with, I just want to be sure."

This is possibly the last thing I need right now. Hearing his voice diffuses my anger and my breath shudders again. I hide behind the curtain and try to swallow the lump in my throat.

"I'll call her."

"Are you home?"

75

Fuse: Origin

"No."

"Where are you?"

"Uh . . . at PT."

"Okay, stay where you are. Don't go anywhere near the Hopman neighborhood, do you hear me? The way the cops are talking on the police scanner, they suspect this is related to the murder you guys witnessed. These thugs could be looking for you, too."

That thought has already crossed my mind, along with a million of other scenarios. It doesn't change my decision. I'm going. Policemen being there will alter my plan, sure, but it won't keep me away.

"Ethan, promise me you'll stay away," Cale persists.

"I promise."

"Good. I'll see you later tonight. Stay safe."

"Okay."

I wipe the few errant tears from my eyes before I emerge from behind the curtain. I pull on the ski mask and my gloves.

Letting out another shuddering breath I say, "Wish me luck."

———

IT'S BEEN ABOUT an hour since I called Emma's phone. I approach the building she's in from a nearby rooftop. There's no telling what I'll find once I'm in there. Emma could be dead, or they could have taken her somewhere else by now.

I try to focus on each step instead of what I'll find. Solve each problem as it comes—the first being catching the bottom rung of the fire escape ladder. It sits six inches above my outstretched hands, even on my tiptoes. It takes three jumps, but I finally get a good grip and slowly pull myself up, feeling my small muscles strain as I do.

Adrenaline keeps me going as I race up the metal fire escape, my feet clanging loudly as I climb to the top. The next problem is, the fire escape only goes to the top window. I jump a few times, but my fingers don't even come close to the edge of the roof of the building.

Chapter Nine

Glancing over the side of the fire escape, I determine how painful it would be if I fell. Three stories up, the fall would seriously maim me, if not kill me. But the clock is ticking and I need to go.

Holding the brick wall for support, I climb up on the edge of the fence of the fire escape and stretch toward the roof line. Still an inch short. With one final look down to the ground, I hop up. My fingers just barely hold the edge.

Swinging my other hand up, I get a better grip and pull myself up the rest of the way. Once I get to the top, my chest heaves and my arms ache, but still I keep going.

The next few buildings are separated only by small alleyways, but still it's a distance of about six feet. Possibly even seven. Adding in the ledge on the edge of the roof, I'm not sure I can make it. But I have to. I've made it this far.

Nervously, I climb up on the ledge and stare down to the bottom again. The police are on their way. I have to get moving.

I hop off the ledge and back onto the rooftop, moving back about ten feet from the edge. With a deep breath, I take off in a sprint, stepping up onto the ledge before vaulting myself forward. Panic sets in while I'm airborne, but I manage to get a grip of the next building's ledge while my body slams into the brick wall. With a bit more effort, I pull myself up.

The building that pinged with the location of Emma's phone is an old factory, connected by several skywalks to nearby buildings. Not wanting to risk being spotted by the cops, I break open the rooftop door and take the stairs down into the building.

It takes awhile for my eyes to adapt to the darkness. Wes chose correctly when making this suit black. Once my eyes have adjusted, it doesn't take me long to find the skywalk to get over to the next building.

Judging by the ancient equipment, this factory used to manufacture plows. Back when Olympia was surrounded by farmland, not suburbia. It's no surprise, either. The Manhattan Expressway sits where a canal ran, allowing quick access for shipping boats.

Most of the old machinery remains, however there are a few

spaces where larger pieces—likely worth more money—have been removed. It's in one of these spaces that I spot something on the lower floor.

Emma's golden hair is splayed out around her, her face pressed against the concrete floor. A small pool of blood escapes beneath her. I watch her for a minute. It's quiet, still. I wonder if her kidnappers have fled.

As I move to get a better look, my foot kicks a loose bolt across the floor, echoing throughout the cavernous factory.

"What was that?" a voice asks.

Another one grunts, "I don't know."

She's definitely not alone. I need to get down to her. I watch as Emma's hair sweeps the dirty floor as they pick her up to move her.

I take off in a run down the metal platform. Against the far wall is a winding staircase leading down to the ground floor. I zip down it as fast as I can, but before I'm even able to step onto the concrete, I get a fist right in my gut.

I double over in pain, wondering if I'm going to vomit. A pair of hands push me flat on the ground.

"C'mon, let's go!" the one holding Emma shouts.

The other guy delivers a kick to my side and then flees with his friend.

I empty my stomach on the floor and force myself to stand. I'm only able to take shallow breaths, but I manage.

Holding my palm out, I try, for the first time since I let loose on Emerson Bluffs, to push the electricity through my palms at my will. Whether it's the suit or it's my determination, I'm rewarded with a long string of lightning that strikes one of the vacant machines on the second floor.

"What the hell was that?" one of them asks the other.

I try again, this time hitting the door they're about to exit out of.

"Leave the girl!" I try to shout in the deepest voice I can manage.

"Fuck off!"

I fire another streak of lightning, and my body noticeably

weakens. I haven't had the suit on for long. It hasn't siphoned off enough electricity to keep me going.

That last streak hits a pit of oil, igniting immediately. I catch of glimpse of the men's faces. They toss Emma aside like she's garbage and take off out the scorched door.

Despite the pain in my abdomen, I run to Emma and pull her away from the fire. Her pants are off. God only knows where they are. Bruises cover the inside of her thighs as well as her neck. Likely from attempted strangulation.

I pull off my mask, and the tears begin to flow again. She was innocent, minded her own business, and they took her and used her. Broke her. In this moment I want nothing more than to strangle them. Punch them over and over again until they're drowning in their own blood. But that won't even do half of the damage that they've done to her. They deserve worse.

I brush her hair from her face, which has no color except for a few red marks. I check for a pulse and am relieved to feel one. Faint, but it's there.

I wipe away the snot from my nose, then kiss the back of her hand and fight to keep my composure. I fail. Miserably.

"The police are on their way," I tell her, though I know she can't hear me. "They've got an ambulance and they're going to take care of you."

The sound of police sirens is louder now. They must be right outside the door. It breaks my heart, but I know I can't stay. "I've gotta go. I'm going to come see you as soon as I can."

Standing, I look down at her. She's twisted like a pretzel on the ground. Bruised, bloody, and still. All I want to do is scoop her up and take her away from here.

On the opposite side of the building, the doors crash in.

"Police!" they shout.

They must've seen the two perverts run out the door and figured it was safe to come in. Hostage situations are generally handled more delicately than this. Hopefully there are police out the door waiting to catch those bastards.

I find a ladder up to the platform leading to the next building. I sprint up to the roof and find a corner to keep out of sight

Fuse: Origin

until the commotion has died enough to go home.

The way she lay there will forever be burned in my mind. She needed me. Someone who could protect her. Instead, I wasted an hour sitting at the clinic. I failed her. I hate myself for it.

Most of all, though, I hate those men. I hate this neighborhood. I hate the Martellis. Sometimes, I even hate this city.

CHAPTER TEN

Emma's still unconscious when I visit her the next morning. She's got a breathing tube down her throat and several monitors hooked up to various parts of her body. The soft beep from the monitor in the corner is the only indication that she's even still breathing.

Her sister, Theresa, is sitting by her side.

"Hi," I mutter when I enter.

"Ethan." She stands and gives me a quick hug. "How are you?"

I shrug. "All right, I guess. How're you?"

She slides her hands in her back pockets and sighs. "I'm working through it."

"Yeah. How is she?"

Theresa turns back to her sister. "Well, the doctors say that she was unconscious when the paramedics got there, and she has severe internal bleeding. Several broken ribs, fractured skull. They're not sure what impact all of this has had on her brain."

I gulp and nod. The sight of her lying comatose in a hospital bed is a lot to take in, but the details of what they did to her are almost too much.

Fuse: Origin

"Have you been here awhile?" I need to change the subject. Facing Theresa now so my back is to Emma, I try to fill my mind with something else—*anything* else.

She nods. "Yeah. My parents were with her last night. They're getting a hotel room a few blocks away and they wanted me to stay with her. When did you hear about all of this?"

I clear my throat. "Um, last night." No use lying to her.

"Oh." There's disappointment in her voice.

"Yeah." I take in a deep breath and look at the floor. "It's been . . . hard."

She nods. "I know. For me, too."

We linger a moment before I say, "Well, it was nice seeing you again."

She looks up at me. "You're not going to stay?"

I breathe in a long shuddering breath before responding, my eyes glued to Emma. "I just can't stand seeing her like this, picturing what they did to her. I can't get it out of my head." I look out the window to avoid her eyes, hoping to pass off the few tears threatening to run down my cheek.

She doesn't say anything. Just rocks on her heels, her arms now wrapped around herself, watching Emma.

"I'll, uh, be back later sometime," I finally say.

"Okay." She nods but keeps her eyes on Emma. She's mad, and I don't blame her. But all of this is too intense for me right now.

I pull myself away from the room and book it to the elevator, trying to keep my composure. I don't know what I'm going to do, but I know I don't want to be surrounded by all these people.

Tucker is on the other side of the elevator doors when they open.

"Ethan, so sorry to hear about your friend."

Not sure whether I can trust my voice, I nod.

"I actually need to talk to you about that. Do you have time to grab a coffee downstairs and answer a few questions?"

It's actually the last thing I want to do, but I hope I can get more answers out of Tucker about what happened last night.

Chapter Ten

How the perverts got their hands on her. What the police know. If they saw me leave.

"Sure, yeah."

The café downstairs is nearly empty. The morning coffee rush has dwindled and there's quiet before the lunch rush.

I take a seat at a rickety metal table while he fetches us a couple of coffees. I don't even like coffee, but I figure I haven't eaten much all day. I need something in me.

"How are you holding up?" he asks as an icebreaker.

"Terribly. Can we just cut to your questions?"

He nods. "Right. The 911 report said you called Emma and a man picked up, correct?"

"Yes."

"What were you calling her about?"

"I got invited to a dinner party for Tranidek Energy. I thought she'd like to come."

The meeting with Frank Rizzoli seems like a lifetime ago. The job offer and his invitation are the furthest things from my mind.

"What did the man on the phone say?"

I sigh, not wanting to relive it. "Something about her screaming, but that they liked it."

"I know it's difficult, but I just need to fact-check everything." He scribbles notes on a pad of paper. "What did you do after the 911 call? Your brother says you got home late."

My heart races. I told Cale I was at PT. If he told Tucker that I said that, our stories won't match. Still, I don't want to start lying to law enforcement. That could get me in worse trouble. "I went to Dr. Fletcher's clinic in Hopman." Cale can be pissed at me if he wants.

"What were you doing there?"

"I wanted to go after them. The arrogance in that man's voice . . . " I shake my head. "I wanted to kill them." The last bit slips out, but it's the truth. Especially after seeing how Emma's doing, I want nothing more than to put those men in the ground.

Tucker looks down at his coffee, neither one of us have taken a sip. "Did you go after them?"

I shake my head. "No. Dr. Fletcher and her friend told me it'd be a bad idea. But I still wish . . . "

He holds up his hand to stop me. "I know."

"How is she?"

"Bad. Did you guys catch the men who did this?"

"We've got two men in custody who were spotted at the scene yesterday. The results of the DNA tests from Emma will help determine their fate."

I shake my head, still in disbelief that all of this is happening. "What happened? How did they get her?"

He hesitates a moment. "This doesn't reach your brother, got it?"

I remain impassive, waiting for him to continue.

"We tracked her cell phone location with the grid. She called a cab from the Wyatt plant and was immediately taken to the crime scene. There was no other activity with her phone until you called."

"They were in the cab?"

"That's what it looks like."

This is still an aftershock from that fucking drive-by. We saw too much, and they want to take out the witnesses. Emma's usually only at the admin building downtown or she's at the plant. They knew where she was headed and she was alone. Me? I was in a meeting in an executive office in Midtown. I could've been right there with her if it were a normal day.

I need to clear my head. I need to prepare for the inevitable attack. If the Martelli family did this to Emma, I can only imagine what they'll do to me. It's coming, and I need to be prepared.

———

IT'S MY FIRST day back at physical therapy since Dean blew up at me. I'm nervous to hear what he has to say but determined to keep pushing myself. One punch knocked me to the ground. If I were stronger, that wouldn't have happened.

I sit in a chair patiently until Dean comes in the room. He closes the door and stares at me with one hand on his hip and

Chapter Ten

the other still on the doorknob.

"I'm sorry for the way I acted the last time you were here," he finally says. "I just didn't want you to hurt yourself. You may think you're fine, but your body might have a different response."

All I do is look at my hands. "It's okay. You were right. I should be more patient." After last night, it seems so insignificant to stay mad for being embarrassed.

He takes a seat across from me and catches my eye. "What's your end goal? Is it just to speed up your recovery, or do you have something else in mind?"

"Self-defense."

"Really? From what?"

I shrug. "It's a dangerous world. I'm a small guy."

He sighs. "Jogging would be a better place to start for beginners. Especially in your case."

I shake my head. "It hurts too much now."

"That's what I was telling you. Chest pains?"

I stand and lift my shirt, showing him the bruises I sport. He's surprised but not put off.

"Who did that to you?" he asks, his hands hovering over my skin.

"Someone in Hopman."

Dean shakes his head. "Man, what are you doing out there? That's a tough place."

"I know." I retake my seat.

He studies me again, running his tongue along his teeth. "All right, here's what I propose: I'll work with you to get you in better shape, but you need to promise me two things."

I roll my eyes and shrug.

"You need to actually listen to me and stick to the regimen I come up with. Pushing yourself too hard will only do more harm than good."

"What's the second?"

"Stay out of places like Hopman. There's nothing good for you there."

"Can't do that."

"Why not? Dr. Fletcher's clinic? I'll talk to her."

Fuse: Origin

I narrow my eyes. "You can't stop me from going to the clinic."

"Okay, fine. But you still need to listen to me."

"Why's that?"

"Well, for one, I'm a professional. I know what I'm doing. And two, my uncle was a boxer. He's the one who got me started in all this." He pats his bicep. "I still hit the sandbag from time to time."

"You're going to teach me how to box?"

"I'm going to teach you how to get away from a brawl without getting your ass kicked." He smiles and I return it. Maybe making some headway in my fitness will help cheer me up. Maybe then I won't feel so powerless.

"Okay, sure. When do we start?"

"Right now." He stands and points to the treadmill.

"Now? What about PT?"

"Think of this as advanced PT."

I'm not sure I'm cut out to be a fighter. But then, what was I thinking when I went out last night? Something needs to change. A little bit of training will only help. Besides, if Dean's going to have me punching things, I think that's exactly the kind of stress relief I need.

Our workout lasts almost an hour. He has me doing interval training to work up my heart strength and make sure it can handle the added stress. My side aches, but I don't tell him. I'm determined to push myself further.

"I'll have to take you to my gym next time," he says as he walks me out. "That way we can start some weight training."

I smile and wipe the sweat from my brow with a towel he lent me. "Yeah, that'd be—"

The TV in the waiting room stops me in my tracks. Mug shots of Emma's rapists flash across the screen. *Suspects say man shot lightning from his hands* scrolls across the bottom of the screen.

Dean follows my gaze. "Bunch of morons, huh? Kidnapping that girl, raping her, and blaming some wizard shocker guy for the reason they just ran right into the cops' arms."

Chapter Ten

"Yeah." I stare into the faces of the men who hurt her. I may have helped get them arrested, but this is far from over. They need to pay the ultimate sacrifice for what they did to her.

CHAPTER ELEVEN

I stretch in bed moments after I wake up. My muscles ache from the hell I put my body through this week. Scratch that. The hell Dean made me put my body through. Within fifteen minutes of our first real workout, I was already regretting allowing him to train me. That man is a beast.

I look at the alarm clock by my bed. It's almost nine in the morning. Ethan and Myra are in the kitchen talking in hushed tones. Surprisingly, they're both still home. From what I can make out through my thin bedroom door, they're talking about me.

"I'll talk to him," she says. "You'll probably just yell at him."

"Well he can't sit around all day. He's been missing a lot of work lately. I can't keep this up for long."

Maybe taking the job at Tranidek is a good idea. Well, it's definitely a good idea, but am I ready to start a new position right now? Then again, giving me something to focus on other than Emma would be good right now. And Wyatt would be filled with her memories.

"I know, but cut him some slack. His girlfriend is in the

88

Chapter Eleven

hospital. Before that, *he* was in the hospital. Just be thankful you don't have to help him with hospital bills."

"I don't even understand why he's acting like this. If it were me, I'd be down there—"

"It's not you. Everyone's different. Let Ethan cope in his own way."

All right. Time for me to get up. Their discussion of me and my feelings is annoying and only firing me up. They're not the ones I should be mad at, but here we are.

With my sore arms, I lift a black T-shirt over my bruised body. I don't want to answer a million questions about the time I played hero.

Myra's sitting alone at the kitchen counter when I emerge from my bedroom. I can hear the water running from the bathroom. I dig through the cupboards and pour myself a bowl of cereal. She looks like she's about to say something, but Cale marches back into the room.

"Hey, look who's up," he says to me.

Myra looks between us. "Um, I'm going to finish getting ready." She slides off the barstool and disappears into the bathroom.

Cale stays where he is, his eyes locked on me.

"Why are you staring at me?"

He clears his throat. "I, uh, need to ask you a question—seriously. And I don't want you to get mad or defensive or anything, I'm just asking."

My eyebrows scrunch together. "What are you talking about?"

"Well, I take it you've seen the news lately."

"About…?"

He sighs. "Ethan, come on. Don't be dense. About that man in black that was spotted in Hopman when Emma…"

I do my best not to react, but I can feel my body tense up. "Yeah?"

"You're not…him, are you?"

I turn away from him to pull the milk out of the fridge. "Why would you say that?"

FUSE: ORIGIN

"Ethan, you were struck by lightning. They claim this man can shoot lightning." He shrugs.

"I was electrocuted."

"When lightning hit your building. Come on, you're splitting hairs here. Just answer the question."

"You're asking if I developed supernatural powers from the lightning strike that left me comatose for a week? And now I use those powers to chase after the men who kidnapped my girlfriend? No, Cale, that's not me."

The skepticism remains on his face, but he puts up his hands. "Okay. Just making sure."

"I can't believe you'd think that."

I need to be more careful. Reading people and seeing through phony stories is part of Cale's job. I know he didn't believe my denial, but hopefully it'll satisfy him for a little bit.

"I had to ask," he says. "The station actually has me doing a piece on him."

"On what? He was seen in passing."

"Exactly, but there have to be witnesses or someone who can give us more details. Basically, I'm reporting on what we know. The problem is, I need to call him something. If I keep calling him the man in black, people are going to think of Will Smith."

I smile. "Um…I don't know. What would be a good name?" I never actually thought I'd get a name for when I was in the suit. Then again, I never thought I'd be running around a dangerous neighborhood at night in tights.

"Well, he shoots lightning from his hands. Maybe Zap-Man or Lucky Strike or something."

I roll my eyes. "Those are dumb."

"Well, you come up with a better idea, then!"

"You could call him the Shocker. Or Fuse."

He rocks his head back and forth. "Those aren't bad. I like Fuse."

Myra emerges from the bathroom.

"What's not bad?" she asks.

"Ethan thinks the man in black should be called Fuse," Cale says.

Chapter Eleven

"Oh, I like that!"

He gathers his things. "I've gotta get going to a meeting." He plants a kiss on Myra's cheek as she retakes her seat at the counter. "I'll see you guys later." He lingers until I look up at him, but he doesn't say anything. Only offers me a sad smile.

Once he's gone, Myra braves the question. "How are you feeling?"

I shrug.

She reaches across the counter toward me. "Do you want me to come with you to the hospital? It's right by city—"

"I really don't want to talk about it."

Sitting up straighter, she says, "Okay."

We sit in silence, the only sound my spoon clinking against the bowl.

"Where's Cale going?" I finally ask.

"You know how he's been chasing after that evening news anchor position? He thinks a big exposé will get him the job." She lets out an exasperated breath of air. "He thinks there's some big corruption going on at the Works."

"So who's he going to meet?" I ask after I finish my cereal.

"One of the engineers on the project. He basically wants to know who authorized construction."

I raise my eyebrows. "Couldn't you point him in the right direction at city hall?"

She sips her coffee. "I could, but I'd rather not use my position as a city councilman's assistant to benefit my reporter boyfriend. That would open up a whole slew of confidentiality issues that I'd rather not get into. Cale's good at his job. He'll find the right people to talk to."

That's what I'm afraid of. City officials pushing through a development project isn't an issue. At least, not one that makes me fearful for Cale. But with everything I know about the Martellis now, it makes me worry he'll find more than he bargained for.

"Besides, Hopman is my district to focus on. With everything that's happened to you and . . . " She trails off, remembering my request not to bring up Emma. "With everything's that happening, I feel like that's a more pressing issue."

FUSE: ORIGIN

"So why doesn't Cale focus on that area?"

"Because everyone else is. He's not going to stand out by following the crowd."

Her words resonate with me. It's as if she knows that's what I need to hear. Even if my outing in the suit wasn't a complete success the first time, it doesn't mean it can't be in the future. I have an ability no one else does. No one else is expecting. I can make a difference.

It's scary. There are risks. Just look at Emma. But I need to take some risks.

———

MYRA INSISTS THAT I go to the hospital. I think she just wants someone from Wyatt to see me there so they know I'm still in mourning and not using her rape as an excuse to play hooky. Still, I procrastinate all day, setting up the new TV Cale bought to replace the one I inadvertently broke, washing the dishes, anything I could think of to put off going to the hospital. By late-afternoon, I had run out of excuses.

Seeing Emma hooked up to those wires, lifeless except for the beeps assuring us her heart is still beating, is the last thing I want to do. Still, I force myself to go. I can't avoid this forever.

Theresa is there when I arrive, and she asks if I can sit with Emma while she picks up her parents from their hotel. I guess they're not used to navigating the city's public transportation. Either that or she still can't stand to look at me after last night.

The only sign of life in Emma are the shallow breaths aided by the piece of plastic shoved down her throat. The bruises on her neck have only gotten darker. Some spots have begun to turn an ugly yellow.

With no distractions, I can feel my emotions consume me. Turmoil, rage, fear. It all leaves me shaking. I lower onto a nearby chair and wipe my face. No tears come, but in their place is a callus I'm not sure will ever soften.

My conversation with Myra this morning only proves that this city is in serious need of a revolution. And not the kind

Chapter Eleven

good-intentioned people like Myra Connors can offer, either. There's only so much she can do from her desk at city hall. No offense to her, but she wasn't on the streets when Emma was attacked. She wasn't there to witness just how cruel some bastards can be.

I hold Emma's hand and sit with her. Doctors and nurses pass by the doorway, but I pay them no mind. I look past all the tubes and wires, through the bruises and scars, and really see Emma. My Emma. It brings a sad smile to my face.

"I'm sorry," I murmur. I feel dumb, but I want her to hear this. "I should've gone there first. Maybe then you'd…" I take in a deep breath and restart. There's nothing I can do about the past. "I'm going to make sure they don't get away with this," I tell her. "The men who did this to you were arrested, and I'm going to make sure they pay for what they did."

I don't know how I'm going to keep that promise, but I do intend to keep it.

I sit and watch her for a long time, replaying memories in my head of us. The stories she'd tell me. The way she told those stories. They make me smile.

Half an hour later, Theresa returns with Emma's parents. It's the first time I've seen them in a while.

"It's good to see you again, Ethan," Emma's father says as he gives me a firm handshake. "How are you holding up?"

I shrug in response.

Emma's mother wears her pain on her face. She offers me a tight hug before moving to Emma's bedside. She stares plainly at her daughter, a million worries likely running through her mind.

"Did the doctor say how she's doing?" Mrs. Landry asks Theresa.

"Yeah." Theresa avoids their eyes. "Dr. McGregory says the results of the various brain scans show hemorrhaging. They've done what they can to ease the pressure, but she's not responding well."

Mrs. Landry leans her head against her husband's chest.

"She'll pull through," he coos.

Fuse: Origin

I stare plainly at Emma, hoping and praying that her father's right. She has to pull through. I need her.

We sit and talk for an hour, discussing the doctor's report, offering each other hope that things will turn out all right. It helps to know that I'm not the only one dealing with this.

On my way back down to the lobby, I consider my choices for going home. Now I have to be careful about where I'm going and when. Overall, crowds are the best thing for me, which is why I decide to walk. My apartment building is off a main street. Even if the sidewalks have cleared for the evening, the streets are still packed with traffic as they move throughout the city.

After I unlock the door, I step into my dark apartment. Cale's keys aren't sitting by the table, so I know he must still be gone. Working late because he went in late, probably.

I leave the lights off and cross the room to my bedroom door, pausing only when I notice it's closed. Clutching the keys that are still in my hand, I try to remember if I closed it this morning when I left. No, I know I left it open.

My chest burns as I begin to panic. I take a deep breath and try to calm myself as I look around for something I can use as a weapon. The closest thing I can find is the broom wedged between the fridge and the wall. It's plastic, but it'll have to do.

Silently crossing the room again, I brandish the broom and throw open the door, bracing myself to use my uncontrollable power if need be.

Facing the window, a man with broad shoulders sits on the edge of my bed. My heart beats faster as I try to find my voice.

"Who are you?"

"It's me, Ethan." Dean looks up. "I need to stay here awhile."

Chapter Twelve

Even though I know we're alone, I close the door behind me. "What do you mean you need to stay here awhile? Why? What's going on?" A million possible scenarios flash through my mind.

"Look, it's just for a little while. Until things get straightened out," he pleads.

"How long's a little while?"

He shrugs. "A few days?"

"Okay. What's wrong with your place?"

He glances out the window. In the distance police sirens sound. I wonder if they're related to him. But then, in the last few weeks I've had my fair share of police sirens too.

"I'll explain in the morning. I just need some rest."

As my eyes adjust to the dim lighting, I see the fatigue on his face. His sunken eyes, the droop in his shoulders. It's all magnified by the shadows, but it's still present.

"How did you know where I live?"

"It's all over your medical records."

Of course. I study him a moment longer and let out a sigh.

"Fine. I'll get you set up on the couch."

Shaking his head, he says, "No. The fewer people who know I'm here, the better."

I narrow my eyes. "What kind of trouble are you in?"

"Nothing that's going to affect you."

I open my mouth to retort, but he raises his eyebrows. "Please?"

I was going to spend tomorrow doing some research into Emma's attackers, see how the investigation is going. My last mental health day before I attempt to dive back into a world without Emma.

Dammit, I need to stop thinking about her like she's dead. She's recovering. She could still turn around for us. We could go back to the way things used to be. I just need to make sure those men pay for what they did. The OPD has them, now we just have to wait for their convictions.

Dean shifts his weight. I've been lost in my own head for too long. I let out another exasperated breath. "Okay, then you're sleeping on the floor."

He holds up his hands. "That's fine. Thank you. I really appreciate it. I'll try to stay out of your way."

"I have no idea when my brother's going to be home, so if you need to use the bathroom or anything, now's the time."

I toss some spare blankets on the hardwood floor next to my bed and change while Dean's in the bathroom. We cross paths as I go to brush my teeth, but don't say anything to each other. As I finish getting ready for bed, Cale comes in.

"Hey, how'd your meeting go?" My bedroom door is ajar and the lamp by my bed is on. I can see Dean's shadow move. My back tenses up.

"They're a bunch of spineless pricks!"

I peel my eyes away from my doorway to avoid suspicion. Still, I raise my voice when I ask, "That bad?"

"Nobody down there would give me a fucking answer!" He snatches a beer out of the fridge. "About anything!"

"Maybe there just isn't a story." I linger in the bathroom doorway, trying to keep Cale's attention away from the opposite side of the apartment.

Chapter Twelve

Slapping his hand on the counter, he looks at me. "The Works has been a chemical wasteland for twenty years. The airport didn't even want to pave over it as part of their expansion plans. Now all of a sudden it's suited for residential housing?" He shakes his head. "There's definitely something there. I just need to rethink my strategy."

"I don't even really know the story behind the Works. I just know it's been a hot topic since this project was first proposed."

He takes a seat on the stool at the counter. Relaxed now that he's facing the opposite direction, I take the seat next to him.

"The Works was actually a big part of Olympia's booming industrial economy," he explains. "The Montgomery Works Company was the largest company to occupy the most northern neighborhood of the city limits."

"What did they do?" I ask.

"Batteries. Distributed all over the country. They were huge."

"So what happened?"

"When industries began turning toward alternative energy sources, the demand for the types of batteries Montgomery produced dropped. They were forced to downsize and eventually moved to Terry Lake. They built a smaller facility on cheaper property."

I nod. "Like everyone else, basically."

"Exactly. The problem was, the company left behind a toxic footprint. Larger than any other company in the city, since no one else matched their size."

"Damn. You would've thought environmentalists or someone would've wanted to clean it up or something."

"Some members of city council claim the area *has* been cleaned up. Others think it's still a danger to nearby neighborhoods. The airport and the Wind Tunnel mostly cut it off from the rest of the city, but there is a residential section that shares the same block with the Works."

"How long have those houses been there? Do they even notice any harmful effects?"

He shrugs. "It's hard to say. Montgomery was there a long

time, but it's been twenty years since they left. Something should've happened in that time."

"Probably did."

"That's what I'm thinking too," he says. "The city council members who claim the area has been surveyed and passed by the state's environmental review board have pushed through this housing development for low-income families. Since they're talking poor people, not as many council members are vocal about the dangers this brings to potential residents of the area. The people who live in the houses adjacent to the property aren't developing cancer or other defects, so they think the area directly next to it is fine. I think it's just a matter of drainage. There isn't any. All the toxic chemicals are just sitting in a pool under all that pavement. Only the future residents of this housing development would be affected."

"Are there any public domain documents you can look through?"

"None that offer anything useful. Montgomery Works is a private company, and the housing developer is privately owned as well. Short of stealing old city documents that might not even tell me anything, I'm stuck."

"Hmm. Aren't there any workers from Montgomery who worked at that site that you can talk to? Maybe get some eyewitness accounts of the practices going on back in the day and report on it daily. Encourage public backlash and put pressure on the developer to cease production."

He chuckles and shakes his head. "If only it were that easy. Just tracking down people like that would take awhile. By then, the project will have started." He takes another sip of his drink. "I don't know. I guess I still have a lot more work to do."

"You'll get it."

"What about you? You going to work tomorrow?"

I look down, silent. If he knew what's been going through my mind—where I *actually* was the night Emma was attacked—he'd have me on the first train out to Mom and Dad's.

"Ethan, what's happened to her is horrible. I'm sorry that you're going through this. But in all fairness, you weren't the one who was attacked. She was. Now I understand that you're more sensitive than I am and you need to mourn her—"

And just like that, he's lost my interest in his argument. When he doesn't understand someone else's reasoning, he immediately belittles and discredits them. As his only brother, I've been the focus of his criticism my whole life.

"—but you have to get on with your life," he continues. "She's not dead."

I chew on my bottom lip while I fight away the demons inside me that are threatening to lash out at him. Especially with Dean in the next room, who has no idea that my life is crumbling all because of a fucking drive-by shooting.

I want to tell him how I found her. The bruises, the blood, the smug looks on the bastards' faces. The way I turned my back on her and left her bleeding, broken, and exposed on the cement floor like an animal.

But I can't. That would put me there that night, and as far as he knows, I wasn't.

"Good night," is all I can manage.

———

ALEX JUMPS WHEN she sees me in the basement of the clinic the next morning. I snuck out early, which worked out perfect because my new roommate had to go to work anyway.

I've got a lot to do today. A lot to look into. A lot to make up for. I needed to get an early start.

"You scared me," she says. "How long have you been here?"

"Got here about six thirty." I keep my eyes on the screen.

"How did you get through the alarm?"

"Wes gave me the code."

She lets out an annoyed breath of air.

"I spruced up your processor on this computer," I add. "The speed on this thing was embarrassing."

"Well, to be fair, it was just in storage until Wes pulled it out when we were testing you. Which, by the way, we should probably continue. Are you still shocking people?"

Fuse: Origin

The tingling in my fingers returned a few days ago. Prior to that, they felt normal. It's probably time to put on the suit again to help regulate the electric discharges from my body.

"Not as much."

"Well, I'd still like to run another neuro test." She leans forward, reading the computer screen. "What are you doing?"

"I've pulled up the arrest report for Emma's attackers from the Olympia Police Department."

"Did you find anything worthwhile?" she asks with a hint of disdain.

I point to a man with short-cropped hair. "This guy is George Kingston. He's in his midthirties. Previous arrests include possession of narcotics last year and breaking and entering from two months ago."

Alex shrugs. "So he's got a record. How is that helping you or the case against him?"

I hold up my finger and bring up another tab. "The other records I've found on him show that he was married for two years. The original petition for divorce claimed that he was abusive, but evidently nothing further came from that claim."

"Of course not," she mutters. "Weren't there two of them? What about the other guy?"

"Mr. Aiden Lipinski. He's actually only two years older than me, if you can believe it."

The image I bring up shows a man with patchy skin and puffy eyes. His nose is an irritated red, and the rest of his face sags.

Alex screws up her face. "Well, he's a looker."

"Extensive drug use will make you look twenty years older."

"What's his record like?"

I pull up yet another tab and skim my findings. "He's been in and out of jail since his days in juvie, as well as various rehabs—clearly none of them worked. He completed his most recent rehab stay six months ago, although he continued to be on probation. I guess now that he can't do drugs, he decided to be a pervert instead."

"Well, at least it sounds like both of them will get put away one way or another," Alex says.

Chapter Twelve

I shake my head. "They need to be put away now."

Both of these men are disgusting. They deserve the worst punishment imaginable. And yet, I'm afraid they might go free.

Theresa said they used a rape kit on Emma, but DNA isn't always conclusive. And even if I was willing to say that I was there, I didn't actually see them touching her. My testimony would mean nothing.

And okay, they walked right out to the police and were promptly arrested, but just like Emma and I were at the shooting that kick-started all of this, they could claim they were just at the wrong place at the wrong time. And until Emma is conscious enough to testify, there's nothing I can find that further indicates they're the perpetrators.

"What more can you do?" She pulls some files from the cabinet beside me.

"A lot more than most people can."

Alex snaps her head to me. "Ethan, you need to stop. This is a dangerous road you're going down. You could end up in a hospital bed right next to her. Is that what you want? Just let it go."

"I can't! I was *there*! I *saw* them!" I point to the fading bruise on my face. "Fucking Aiden Lipinski nearly knocked me out."

"So what are you going to do about it?" she fires back.

"What I should've done the last time."

"You're going to play God and kill two men?"

I turn back to the computer and mutter, "It wouldn't be the first time."

She pulls on my shoulder and spins me toward her. "Ethan, take a look at yourself. Is this the kind of man you want to be? Is this someone who would make Emma proud? Because, let me tell you, you are not the person I met in the hospital."

"Things have changed. I've changed. I'm sorry if that offends you, but I can't let them get away. I've got an opportunity to get justice for her. Doesn't she deserve that?"

Alex bites her lip and lets out a breath.

"I've already talked to Wes," I say when I turn back to the computer. "He called me after my first outing in the suit, asking how it worked. He said he's got an idea for a new suit worked up

101

that will better accommodate the charges running through my body." I turn back and stare blankly at the scream, then mutter, "Like it or not, this is who I've become."

She studies me a moment longer before turning toward the stairs without a word.

Tossing my head back against the chair, I rub my hand in my face. I was harsh, I know that. She has a point. If I keep going like this, I'm going to drive myself crazy. I'm already halfway there. Before I leave today, I'll have to apologize to Alex. She's sticking out her neck for me. I need to remember that.

The next link I pull up is the website of the *Olympia Tribune*. Under the police blotter, the headline reads, "Pair arrested for rape released on bail."

———

THE RESEARCH ON the two men led me down a rabbit hole into the Martelli crime family and mafias in general. In a crime family, there are typically several tiers in the hierarchy. Kingston and Lipinski were what Wikipedia defined as "associates." The ones who got their hands dirty but weren't full-blown members of the family.

No, the man who's truly responsible for this is higher up in the food chain. The caporegime who controls the south side of town is the one who is most likely to have put the hit on us. Sure, he may have consulted with the family boss, but ultimately, it was the capo who ordered his men to beat and rape Emma.

Her attackers are the only connection I have, though. Even if they don't know why, they'll know who sent them. I have to start there.

My stomach gurgles loudly on my way home. I haven't had much to eat all day. I grabbed a banana on my way to the clinic this morning and had a couple bottles of water, but other than that, I've got nothing in me.

That, coupled with the clinic closing for the night, is the reason I'm on my way home now. Good thing tomorrow's Saturday. I'll have more time to look into the Martellis before I go to that

Chapter Twelve

fancy dinner at Frank Rizzoli's. I just wish I hadn't already told him that I'd be there.

Dean is leaning on the wall near the front door of my building when I approach.

"It's about time," he says.

"Hey, I'm doing *you* a favor. I don't want to hear you complaining." I pull out my key and unlock the door. "What are you doing down here anyway? Is Cale upstairs?"

I hold the door open for him but he doesn't move.

"I just need to ask you one question before we go up there."

I roll my eyes. I'm so tired of having to explain myself to everyone. Hopefully next week when I'm back to work everyone will get off my back about my every move.

"Are you that guy they were talking about on the news the other day? The one who shoots lightning out of his hands?"

CHAPTER THIRTEEN

As hard as I try to maintain a cool demeanor, I know I probably look at least a little dumbfounded.

I was with him when reports of the lightning man first hit the news. Like Cale, he probably put the clues together. It's not rocket science. The lightning strike is the only reason I know Dean at all. Not to mention the shocks he gets during PT.

"I didn't mean to pry," he continues in my silence. "I was looking for a towel for the shower and found what I thought was a Halloween costume." He shrugs. "I don't know. Maybe it is. It's just—it had the lightning bolt, and I remembered your scar and what happened to you and what was on the news."

Subconsciously, I reach for my scarred arm. Dean and I left together this morning. That means he found it when I was still home and didn't say anything. He's been thinking about this all day.

He shakes his head. "It's stupid. Never mind. I didn't mean to get all in your business. I can find a new place to stay if you want."

My mind is still racing. I should've left the suit back at the clinic, but after I found Emma, I wasn't thinking straight. Actually, I never took the suit off until I got home. I had it stashed in my closet, so it makes sense that Dean found it. And if he could find it, then so could Cale. My brother is already suspicious.

I consider lying to him, but anything I come up with now would be so obviously fake that it'll create suspicion. Just like it did with Cale. The difference is, Dean is less likely to lecture me about being careful. Depending on what kind of trouble he's in, it'd be better not to put an even bigger target on my back. Better to explain to him why he needs to keep it quiet.

"You don't have to go anywhere else." I tilt my head toward the door. "Come on. I'll explain."

The scent of cologne wafting from the bathroom tells me Cale is still home when we head up.

"Hey," he calls to me. "Myra and I are heading to dinner in a bit. I'm working at the library in the morning so I'll probably just stay at her place."

"Okay," I call back.

Dean looks uncomfortable, but I point to the barstool by the kitchen counter. No sense in sneaking around. For all Cale knows, Dean's just hanging out. He doesn't have to know he's staying here.

Just as I'm handing Dean a glass of water, Cale emerges from the bathroom. He's wearing a navy blue sweater with a plaid button-up underneath and khakis.

"Oh, hey. I didn't realize you brought someone over." My brother extends his hand. "I'm Cale, Ethan's brother."

"Dean. Nice to meet you."

"He's my physical therapist," I add. "And he's been working with me at the gym, too."

Cale's surprised. "The gym?"

At the moment, that's all the confession I'm willing to dole out.

"Yeah, I just started going. Dean's been helping me because I have no idea what I'm doing."

"Just don't hurt yourself." He takes the seat next to Dean and pulls on his shoes.

FUSE: ORIGIN

"Where are you going to dinner?" I ask, trying to act as casual as I can, even though my nerves are eating me up.

"Valentino's or something. It's right downtown on the waterfront."

Cale and Myra can afford to go to the classier places from time to time. I guess this is Cale's way of celebrating not having to shoulder the rent all on his own anymore now that I'm back at work. Well, up until a few days ago . . .

"Tell Myra I said hi," I say as he grabs his keys from the hook.

"Will do. Nice meeting you, Dean." Cale points to me. "Go easy on him. He's just a little guy."

Deafening silence fills the room after Cale leaves. I listen to the sound of his footsteps down the hallway and the bang of the staircase door.

"So," Dean starts.

"So."

He lifts his eyebrows. "Are we going to talk or just sit here and stare at each other?"

I let out a deep breath of air but don't feel any better. "Right. Well, um . . . what do you want to know?"

"Start from the beginning."

I lean back on the counter and cross my arms. "Okay, well you know I was struck by lightning." I pull back my sleeve and show him my scar.

"Yeah."

I hesitate, trying to figure out the best way to tell him what I can do. I just decide to spit it out, in all its ridiculousness. "Well, according to Dr. Fletcher and her colleague, my body mutated. Since the strike I've been, uh, generating electricity."

"What do you mean?"

"I'm basically a power plant. I can't control it that well, but Dr. Strider says that I can learn how."

"Oh." He draws out the word. "So that's why you're constantly zapping me during therapy."

I nod. "You probably think I'm crazy. But it's real."

He nods slowly. "All right."

Yup, he definitely thinks I'm crazy.

Chapter Thirteen

"So," he continues, "you're being studied?"

Rocking my head back and forth I say, "Sort of. After the week in the hospital, I spent three weeks being the test subject for Dr. Fletcher at her clinic in Hopman. That led me to two weeks ago. My girlfriend Emma and I were walking back from Wyatt's solar panel plant when we watched a guy get his head blown off during a drive-by."

His mouth drops. "Wait a minute, Emma's the girl from the news?"

I nod. "We saw the shooter. According to the police, he was a member of the Martelli family. I guess we're marked because of that."

"What do you mean?" Dean sits up straighter and takes a sip of his water.

"They didn't shoot the witnesses, so they wanted to cover their tracks. I nearly got my ass kicked outside of the clinic, but I—" The fact that I killed a man is still too much to confess just yet. He asked if I was the man in the suit, not if I have any blood on my hands.

"You . . . ?"

"Um, my powers took care of it."

He raises his eyebrows again, but doesn't say anything. "That's rough, man."

I shake my head. "Except they got Emma. They couldn't get to me and they were pissed, so they went after her." I bite my bottom lip, trying to keep my voice steady, but it's no use. "What they did to her . . . And now they're out on bail."

"How do you know?"

"I read it online. The fuckers are lying and saying they didn't touch her when I saw them there that night!" I wipe away the moisture from my face, embarrassed and angry.

"Okay."

"Okay what?" I ask, harsher than I mean.

"Okay, what are we going to do from here?"

I shrug. "I don't know. I was reading up on crime families, and those men probably don't even know why they were doing what they were doing."

"No, they're just associates."

"And how would you know?"

Dean shakes his head. "The mafia's been in Olympia for a while."

"Right."

"So what are you going to do now?"

"I figured the guy who ordered the attack is probably the Hopman caporegime. I just need to find out who he is, and then I'm going to take him down."

His eyes are wide. "I'd be careful with that. These are powerful men. You never know who's in the family and who isn't. It's the twenty-first century. It's hard to find pure Sicilian-descended Italians anymore. They've accepted more people into their circles. At least, that's what I've heard."

I nod again. "Right."

"So what do you mean by 'take down'? Are you talking . . . ?" He slides a finger across his throat.

"That'd be a last resort."

"Can you do that? With your powers, I mean."

Turning toward the window, I confess, "Yes, I can."

Through the reflection in the window, I can see Dean watching me, but he doesn't say anything.

Something isn't adding up with Dean's story. There's a reason he's sleeping on my floor. Not to sound completely selfish, but I have enough problems of my own without getting involved in his. And yet, I haven't told him to leave.

Maybe it's because he may know more than he's letting on and can help me, or maybe it's my incessant need to be the nice guy, but I have no intention of kicking him out. Plus it's a relief to talk to someone about everything I'm going through without getting a lecture.

"Do you know their names?" he asks.

I nod. "Yeah. That's what I was doing today. George Kingston and Aiden Lipinski. I have no idea how to find them, though."

"Well, they've probably been arrested before, right?"

I nod. "That's what I found, yeah."

Chapter Thirteen

"Then they each have a record, meaning their addresses would be listed."

"What if they're not current?"

"It's a start. You should be able to find them online."

"Well, I stumbled upon a couple of reports for Lipinski . . . " I get up and fetch my laptop from my room.

"You hungry?" he asks.

I glance at the stove. "Yeah. I just don't feel like making anything. We could order out if you want."

"I can make something. If you don't mind, that is."

I scrunch my eyebrows. "You want to make me dinner?"

"I'm hungry."

A grin spreads across my face. "Okay, knock yourself out."

I take his seat at the counter and he goes to the fridge and we both get to work. He moves around the kitchen like a pro. I have to point out where we keep a couple things, and he needs to improvise a bit with our limited pantry, but he manages.

Meanwhile, I dive into the corners of the internet to find the police report I brought up back at the clinic this morning. Retracing my steps would be easier if I only had to sift through my browsing history, but by the time Dean's placing a heaping plateful of pasta with a homemade white sauce in front of me, I've found it.

He takes the seat next to me and says, "I just couldn't use canned sauce. My mother would've rolled over in her grave." He glances at my screen. "You find it?"

"Yeah. According to this he lives out on Montgomery Avenue by the airport." I dig in to my plate.

"That's not surprising for someone of his stature."

Montgomery Avenue is one of the streets that runs through the Works. There's a small strip of row houses between the airport and the Wind Tunnel that are still rented out as apartments. Between the noise of the two borders, the only ones willing to live there are the ones who are desperate.

"So what do we do now?" I ask.

"You've got the suit, right?"

"And do what?" I ask.

Fuse: Origin

"Find out who sent him. He might not know why he was ordered to hurt your friend, but he definitely knows *who* told him to."

My chest tightens with apprehension. Last time I saw Lipinski, he sacked me right in the gut. I've only been to the gym twice since then; I'm not any stronger. Certainly not any more confident.

"Do you want me to come with you?" Dean asks.

I twist my fork in my pasta. "You probably should."

He nods and takes another bite. "Okay. But I'll have to wait outside. I don't have a mask."

I smile. "Deal."

The rest of our conversation at dinner is still polite, but more friendly than we've been. I tell him about my brother and Myra and what they do for a living. I tell him about my parents and their fear of the city. I tell him about Emma. How we met. What she's like. I'm careful to stay away from the topic of the attack.

On the flip side, he talks mostly of his late mother. From the few stories he shares, she sounds like she was a no-nonsense, headstrong woman who took care of her family, especially Dean. From what I've gathered, he was a little bit of a mama's boy. But then, with no other siblings, she must've been very protective of him.

———

IT SHOULD'VE REALLY come as no surprise that Dean has a motorcycle. It just fits his personality. But it's not the most stealthy vehicle. Still, the ride distracts me enough to alleviate my nerves as we head toward Aiden Lipinski's apartment.

Before we left, Dean ran through our game plan. He'll stop long enough for me to hop off the bike and get inside, then circle around to give me time to take Lipinski by surprise and him time to scope out any potential gunmen protecting Lipinski. Once I'm done finding out who sent him, Dean will be waiting outside.

The element of surprise is my biggest asset here. Not to

Chapter Thirteen

mention the fact that I'm counting on this being Lipinski's current address. Hopefully he's home alone and unarmed.

We roll up to the dilapidated row of townhouses wedged between the airport and the Wind Tunnel. The roar of airplanes and traffic means this place is never quiet.

I hop off the bike and Dean mutters, "Good luck," before rolling away.

Creeping close to the building to avoid being seen through any windows, I locate number seven and walk up the few steps to the front door, which is unlocked.

I step into the living room that's open to the kitchen in the back of the house. The TV glow allows me to see that the place is littered with garbage, oversized ratty furniture, and other clutter. But my eyes are drawn to what's on the makeshift coffee table: bags of white powder. There have to be at least fifty of them.

I hear movement from up the stairs and flatten myself against the wall, praying to God that he's here alone.

The footsteps carry to the top of the staircase and then down to my level. He doesn't notice me in the shadows, hidden with the help of Wes's suit.

I shoot lightning at the TV, snapping Lipinski's attention to me. He lunges across the room, likely for a weapon, but I catch his arm before he reaches it. Slamming him against the wall, I shout in his face, "The girl you raped in Hopman, who told you to do that?"

He stutters. "I…I don't know anything, man. That was just a misunderstand—"

I punch him in the gut. "Don't fucking lie to me!" I growl. His breath is rancid, but I don't move.

"Listen," he groans, "I was just told I could make some money. He said I might be arrested but he'd take care of it. Said I could have some fun and make some extra cash, that's all."

I toss him to the floor, zaps erupting between my fingertips as I stand over him.

"Some fun? You call putting a woman in the hospital fun? You're disgusting." I kick at him but he grabs my foot and drops me to the floor.

Fuse: Origin

We struggle. He tries to keep me at bay long enough to grab his gun from its hiding spot on the other side of the room. I hold off on zapping him. I need him to be able to talk.

"Tell me who sent you and I'll leave." I get to my feet.

He puts up his shaky hands. "Hey man, take it easy."

I fire another string of lightning by him, feeling myself grow more tired. I need to be careful. I haven't had the suit on that long.

"M-Michael! His name is Michael!"

I step forward and grab his yellowing T-shirt. "Last name," I say through gritted teeth.

"He's going to come after me, man," Lipinski whimpers, "if he knows I'm the one who gave up his name."

I shove him back against the wall and slam my fist beside his head. "And what do you think *I'm* going to do to you?"

He gulps and shuts his eyes tight. "Bello. Michael Bello. Said he just needed to tie up some loose ends. That's all I know. I swear!"

I let out heavy breaths, resisting the urge to wrap my hands around this man's neck and squeeze until the light leaves his eyes. Instead, I hear the roar of Dean's motorcycle outside as he returns.

Using all of my willpower, I step away from Emma's attacker and run back out to Dean. I got what I came here for.

———

DEAN EMERGES FROM my bedroom the next day and takes a seat at the counter. Since Cale wasn't home last night, I gave Dean my bed to sleep in. At first he argued, saying he didn't want to displace me from my own bed, but I insisted. Besides, it made more sense for me to sleep on the couch in case Cale came home in the middle of the night. Obviously, that never happened.

I pass Dean the box of Cheerios and a bowl and spoon. "Sleep okay?"

"Great." He pours himself some cereal. "Thanks again. It was nice to be off the floor for one night."

Chapter Thirteen

"No problem." We eat in silence for a bit before I ask, "When do you think it'll be safe to go back to your apartment?"

He shrugs. "I don't know. I'm going to scope it out today."

"Who are you looking for, exactly?"

He studies me while he chews. "Listen, please don't go poking around. The less you know, the better. If anyone asks about me, tell them you haven't seen me."

I want to press him for more answers, but I let it go. Still, I can't help but feel annoyed that I'm trusting him with a secret and he can't do the same with me.

"I think I proved last night that I can handle myself," I say.

"Low-level thugs like Lipinski don't even come close to the type of men who're after me," Dean says.

"Like Michael Bello?" I ask.

Dean rocks his head back and forth. "Not him specifically, but men like him."

"And they're after you beca—"

"We need to talk about Bello," he cuts me off. "What do you want to do?"

I did a bit of research on him last night when I was too wired to sleep. He's a prominent real estate developer in the city. His most famous contributions were building the Lakeside Village condos, which revitalized the area. He also did some work in Midtown.

I shrug. "I'm not sure I even believe what Lipinski said. Bello has business interests elsewhere in the city. Why would he order the retaliation of an attack that happened in Hopman? It doesn't make sense."

"Doesn't it?" Dean asks. "His professional colleagues aren't in Hopman. If he's ordering criminals around there, he's less likely to be recognized. If anyone does spot him, he can hide under the cover of looking for his next big development."

I chew on my lip and consider this. It makes sense. But a part of me still wants Lipinski and Kingston to pay for what they did.

"Okay, so let's say Bello is the guy who ordered them. The scumbags who touched her are still running around."

Dean shakes his head. "Even if you put those two away, the

hit is still out on the both of you. When Emma gets released from the hospital, she's not just going to jump right back into her lifestyle. She's going to be resting at home. Sooner or later her guard will be down and then—"

I hold up my hand. "Okay, I get it. So what do you want me to do?"

Dean rubs his stubbly chin as he thinks. "Let me look into this a bit more and figure something out."

"You'll have the evening to yourself if Cale doesn't come home."

"Why's that?" His cereal bowl obstructs my view of his face as he drinks up his milk.

"I got invited to a dinner party. I was going to ask Emma, but . . . "

"She's going to make it through," he reminds me.

I nod, losing myself in the memory of her. Tonight is going to be unbearable. Emma was supposed to be my buffer from the corporate crazies. Now the crazies will serve as a constant reminder of the fact that I need to go back to work Monday morning without her.

No matter where I work, Wyatt or Tranidek, it'll be without Emma. At least for a little while. Part of me is putting off making a decision about Tranidek in the hopes that Emma will recover and come back to work and everything will be normal.

"Now about our workout for today. If you're going to keep up this superhero stuff, you're going to need to step it up. I'm talking endurance and strength, not to mention the other things that are going to take even longer to learn."

"Like what?" I ask.

He taps the side of his head. "Street smarts. You need to make quick decisions and follow through with them. No amount of weight lifting or miles run will save you from a stupid decision."

"And you're the expert on street smarts?"

"There's a lot about me you don't know."

There sure is.

Chapter Fourteen

I lift my chin up as Cale helps me tie my tie for Mr. Rizzoli's dinner party. I'm wearing the suit I only pull out for weddings. And only fancy weddings, at that.

"I hate this suit," I mutter, eyeing myself in the mirror on my closet door.

"Stop it, you look sharp." Cale tightens the knot and stands back. "Well, look at you!"

I roll my eyes.

"Relax, dude. It's just dinner."

Turning, I look myself over in the mirror. I look tense. Nervous. The suit probably isn't the source of my discomfort.

Actually, I take that back. It's *definitely* not the source of my discomfort. This whole damn dinner is. Butterflies float in my stomach.

"I think I have to pee again," I say.

"You just peed two minutes ago. You're going to be great." He hands me my jacket.

"So, I actually need to talk to you about something." I pull my jacket on and brush off some of the lint from the sleeves.

"What's that? You're not pregnant, are you?"

I shoot him a look and he grins. "You know my friend Dean? The one who's been helping me at the gym?" Funny enough, that's probably where Dean is now.

"Yeah, what about him?"

"His apartment is being renovated and he needs a place to stay for a while." I rehearsed this line in the shower, and I'm surprised by how well I pull it off.

"How long have you known this guy?"

"Not long, but listen, he'll just crash on the couch until he can go back to his place."

Cale crosses his arms and lets out a deep breath. "Okay. Just for a little while."

"Awesome, thanks."

"Yeah yeah. Now come on, you gotta get going."

I glance at the clock. I have twenty minutes to get there. Just barely enough time.

The train ride seems to take forever. I don't often go this far west in the city. I would have guessed that the CEO of Tranidek Energy would have lived along the parkways or in one of the fancy row houses near Broadway, but instead I'm heading over to Midtown. I guess a high-rise penthouse overlooking the Olympia Country Club is more Frank Rizzoli's style. Should've known.

My heart seems to race faster the higher the elevator rises. I wish I wasn't here alone. I don't know any of these people. I should've found someone else to bring, but who? It would've been odd to bring Dean, and bringing my brother was out of the question because, as an investigative reporter, he would've made everyone guarded.

I suppose I just need to man up and get through this dinner. It's just a couple hours out of my life. I can do this.

The elevator doors slide open to reveal the expansive space. And then they threaten to lock me in before I can bring myself to move.

Stepping onto the hardwood floors, I gape at the fifteen-foot floor-to-ceiling windows in the next room. Long white curtains

Chapter Fourteen

extend from the top of the windows to the floor. The beige walls are offset by the dark molding lining the room. Two black leather couches sit facing each other, with a glass coffee table between them. On one side of the room sits a large mirror with an intricate antique-gold frame. The other side of the room is reserved for a grand piano that likely never gets played.

The room opens up on each side to two smaller rooms. Still, each of those is probably bigger than my whole apartment. One is lined with bookshelves and has several plump chairs to relax in with a book. The other room has a long oak table in the center. From the clinking of glasses and silverware, I figure it's the dining room.

"Mr. Pierce! Welcome!" Mr. Rizzoli greets me with a smile on his face and a glass of champagne in his left hand. He shakes my hand vigorously—likely basking in my peasant wonder of his home—and leads me into the dining room.

"I'd like you to meet some of my other guests."

Two men appear from around the corner with one woman, who I presume is one of their wives. One is tall and blonde, wearing a gray suit coat and brown loafers. The other man is shorter and rounder, with a black suit and a gold ring on each of his ring fingers. The thin woman wears a modest black dress with a white sweater.

"This is Michael Bello," Mr. Rizzoli introduces the couple in the black outfits, "and his wife, Maria."

My mouth suddenly goes dry and I feel a heat wave over my entire body. I could kill him right here. Just open my palm and zap him until he's no longer breathing—but I can't. I'm not a murderer. Not intentionally, anyway.

I choke down my burning hatred for Mr. Bello and shake each of their hands.

"Frank has told us your story," Maria tells me. "How inspiring!"

"Yeah, I guess so. I'm just happy to be breathing."

Apparently I'm better at this than I thought, because all four of them burst out laughing.

Emma would have helped relieve some of these nerves

simply by being another normal person. Someone who has to go to work each day in order to maintain a modest living. These people could stop working for a year and would still be making money from investments and stocks and trust funds.

"And this is Leon Wallace."

Once I've been introduced, Mr. Rizzoli continues. "I'm sure you've heard of both these men in the news."

I have. Leon Wallace is also a land developer who is capitalizing on Olympia's rebound. Each of them have invested millions of their own dollars into the city and brought in even more investments from outside sources.   One of them also just happens to be a white-collar criminal. I wonder what kind of friendship Mr. Rizzoli and Bello have.

"Mike has a few towers going up down on the waterfront near Lakeside Village," Mr. Rizzoli explains. "He's actually the one who helped fund this building, as well."

Mr. Bello looks down at the floor shyly until Rizzoli moves on. Oh, how modest. I stare blankly, but inside I'm rolling my eyes.

"And Leon is tackling probably one of the worst parts of the city: the Works."

My mind flashes to Cale. I wonder if I'll be able to get some sort of contact information for him. But then, even if I did, there's no guarantee that Wallace would tell Cale anything. Especially if my brother's implying that he is cutting some serious corners and putting people at risk.

"Yup," Wallace says with a nod. "We're putting in three or four blocks of single-family homes for people who are struggling financially. It'll help reinvigorate the city from north to south."

Oh, what a saint.

Well, no. That was uncalled for. Cale hasn't found out anything yet. I can't write Wallace off for it. Besides, I just got here. I still have to endure dinner with them. No sense in damning them this early in the evening. But if the Works—which sits just north of Lipinski's house—is anything like what I saw last night, the project is doomed from the start.

Rizzoli gives us a tour of the house, name dropping at every chance, but mostly place dropping.

"The marble was imported from Italy," he says in the bathroom, which is twice the size of my kitchen. "The rug is Egyptian," he says in the master bedroom.

The small collection of photos in one of the guest bedrooms shows not only a fit Rizzoli at several beaches but also his yachts. Yes, plural.

"This is from when I took a couple business associates of mine on a cruise in Greece. I can't remember if it was last summer's cruise or the summer before that. We went again in the fall, but it was too chilly."

By time the tour ends, the catering staff are laying out the first course. I can't stand to break bread with the man who ordered Emma's attack. With Rizzoli at the head of the table and Maria taking the seat next to her husband, I sit next to Wallace. Initially, I think it'd be perfect to try to get something out of him for Cale, but it quickly becomes apparent that Rizzoli is going to lead the conversation throughout dinner.

We hear stories about his trips around the world, about how he's gotten to where he is today with his career, more details about his house, and how his "whore" of an ex-wife is still making bank from him with alimony checks. I sit quietly and smile and nod a lot.

Luckily, the food is good, even if a little too filling. I should've expected a three-course meal. After this morning's workout with Dean, my body is ready for some nourishment. Still, my stomach can only hold so much.

"I heard there are no new leads on the masked man," Wallace says to Bello, and my ears perk up.

"No, he basically just disappeared," Michael says, cutting into his food. "They were more focused on making sure that girl was all right."

"What happened?" Maria asks.

Bello waves his hand. "Probably just a drug deal gone wrong. I don't know if the doctors found any drugs in her system, but I'm sure she wasn't completely innocent."

My blood boils. That's exactly what she was. Innocent. Bello, of all people, knows this.

"Wasn't the guy in the suit trying to save her?" I ask with an edge to my voice.

Everyone looks up at me.

Finally, Bello breaks out into a laugh. "If that's what he was doing, he did a hell of a job!"

"It was the first sighting of him," I add. "Maybe he's new."

"Then he's going to realize he's in way over his head," Bello counters. "Hopman isn't a place for amateurs."

I've lost my appetite. All I want to do is jump across the table and strangle him, but I can't. I'm trapped.

Sensing the tension, Rizzoli redirects the conversation. "Reminds me of growing up in New York. There were parts of the city that were horrible . . . "

After dinner, the servers set out coffee in the library and we move there. Bello and his wife excuse themselves to the balcony, leaving me, Rizzoli, and Wallace alone.

"What did you think of the meal, Mr. Pierce?" Rizzoli asks.

"Very good. Thanks again for inviting me." I slowly sip my coffee. I don't want it, but I don't want to be rude.

"You should bring a lady friend next time."

I nod, wondering whether he knows my intent was to ask Emma to come. But then, how would he? He's the top executive at one of the biggest companies in the city. Up until a month and a half ago, Emma and I were both tech support.

"You don't say much, do you, kid?" Wallace asks.

Before I have a chance to retort, Rizzoli waves his hand to me. "Leon, please. He's a guest, just as you are. Have some respect. Besides, I admire his silence." He looks at me. "You're an observer, a listener."

"Actually," I say, "Mr. Wallace, I was hoping I'd be able to speak to you about your new development with the Works."

"It's too late for business." He turns to Rizzoli. "Mind if I enjoy a cigar?"

With his coffee mug in hand, Rizzoli motions to the door leading to the balcony. "Outside."

With a huff, Wallace exits through the glass door. Once he's

Chapter Fourteen

gone, Rizzoli addresses me. "You're interested in the city's redevelopment?"

I shrug, trying to act casual. "Well, Olympia is my home. I'm just curious. I read all the time about Mr. Bello's developments."

He nods slowly. "Yes. The *Tribune* has decided that high-rises are more newsworthy than low-income housing."

"With all due respect, the Works is having some difficulty."

Rizzoli chuckles and sets his mug on the table between our chairs. "I was right about you." He wags a finger at me. "You pay attention. I like to surround myself with people such as yourself."

Reflexively, I scrunch my eyebrows in confusion but immediately smooth them out when I realize what I'm doing. "What do you mean?"

"If I'm being honest, the first time I heard your name I thought you'd be a liability to the company if you were my employee. I thought for sure you or your family would sue Wyatt for your accident. But then I began to look into who you were, and I just knew you could be an asset.

"I knew I wanted you to come work for Tranidek, but I didn't want you to be swayed by a large paycheck. I've been in charge of employees for a long time. Workers tend to do better when they're truly passionate about their job. If you were going to come work for me, I wanted to make sure you wanted it."

Which is why they paid my hospital bills.

"You know what this dinner was really about?" he asks.

I shake my head.

"Think about it: my colleagues, myself, and you—we each have such passion for this city. A lot of people do, but unlike them, we're all in a position to do something about it."

"I don't mean to be rude, but why are you so invested in Olympia? You grew up in New York City."

He smiles. "Well, I consider myself a transplant. Since joining this company, I've seen vast improvements throughout the city. And what's good for Olympia is good for Tranidek. This company will have veins running through the streets of this city! With your help, of course. We can be the future of Olympia, and I want you to be a part of that."

FUSE: ORIGIN

I sip my coffee.

"Have you given any more thought to my proposal from the other day?"

Only a little, but nothing serious. Not with everything that's happened with Emma and finding out Bello is behind all this. Does Rizzoli know that? Would I end up having to work with the man who ordered Emma's rape just to put food on the table?

"Not much," I finally say. "I've had a lot going on, and it's a big decision."

He nods. "Of course, yeah. Think about it and let me know. I would like to get you into training as soon as possible."

CHAPTER FIFTEEN

Cale's in bed by the time I get home just after ten. The apartment is dark and quiet, except for the faint sounds of the TV coming from his bedroom.

Dean's sitting in the living room with the *Tribune* spread across his outstretched legs. The lamp in the corner is the only thing on.

"Don't you need more light?" I ask.

He pulls in his legs and starts folding up the paper. "No, this is fine."

Following me into my room, he leans against the doorway as I lay the garment bag for my suit on my bed and place the jacket and tie over it. Kicking off my shoes, I return them to the bag too.

"How'd your dinner go?" Dean asks quietly.

"Long." I unbutton the dress shirt and toss it in my hamper, freeing my arms for the first time in a couple hours. "Did I ever tell you I got offered a job at Tranidek?"

"No! When did that happen?" His bright white teeth contrast with his olive skin.

"Last week. I met with the CEO of the company—the one who's paying my bills." I rummage through my dresser and pull out clothes for bed. "He wants me to help develop software for the solar roadways that's better than Wyatt's. They want to cut a deal with Wyatt and install at least some of the new roadways."

"Oh damn. So you'd be jumping ship."

I nod. "Yeah, pretty much."

"How did you manage to meet the CEO?"

Shrugging, I say, "His assistant called me. Said Mr. Rizzoli wanted to speak with me personally."

"Rizzoli?" Dean stiffens up. "What's his first name?"

"Frank. Why, do you know him?"

"Frank Rizzoli?" His voice jumps.

I shoot him a look. "Yeah, why?"

"Oh, Ethan," he says in a hushed voice.

"Does this have to do with Michael Bello? He was there tonight too."

Fear spreads across his face. "This is not good."

"I know."

He shakes his head. "No, if you think Bello is dangerous, Rizzo doesn't even compare."

"Rizzo? What are you talking about?"

"Just trust me."

I shake my head. "Enough. If you expect me to trust you—and to let you stay here—you need to tell me more than that."

The floor suddenly fascinates him and he studies it. Just as I'm about to forget it and head to the bathroom to get ready for bed, he speaks up.

"You're right. But what I'm about to tell you is serious."

Absently, I look at the scar on my right arm. "And mine isn't?"

"I didn't say that."

"So what are you saying?"

"A couple years ago I got into it with my father. He threw me out and I . . . I had nowhere to go. Broke, living on the streets. I was begging people for food, scaring them off because I hadn't taken a shower in weeks."

Chapter Fifteen

I divert my eyes, feeling like my life has been spoiled compared to his. Who am I kidding? My life *was* spoiled compared to his. That is, if he's telling the truth. But for whatever reason, I let him talk. I can't explain it, but I trust him.

"One man took me in," he continues. "James Alexander. Brought me into his home. Let me shower, gave me a fresh set of clothes and a nice hot meal. I was so grateful that I wanted to repay him somehow."

My mind races with the millions of things he could've done, but somehow I know.

"It started with small things. Wait for someone on the corner of Sherman and West Streets to get a package and bring it back home. Or pick up some guy from a random address. It didn't seem like a big deal at the time, but I guess I was a good worker."

I have so many questions: Who were some of these men? Didn't he consider telling the police? What about trying to patch things up with his father? Is he still in touch with these men now? Are they the ones he's hiding from? Are they going to come after me and Cale if they find him? Will Cale end up like Emma?

Instead, I seal my lips and let him continue. It takes a minute, but he does.

"Things escalated. One of the men I was picking up was gunned down as he was getting in the car. Blood splattered all over. Inside the car, all over me. I was scared, so I drove off. Jamie was pissed. Said I should've ditched the car somewhere and gotten the blood off me and my clothes."

"Is that why you're here?"

He shakes his head. "They called Frank, who told me to take care of it or it could be trouble for me."

"Frank Rizzoli?"

He nods.

"How involved is he?" Maybe that's why Mr. Rizzoli is interested in me switching to Tranidek. Does he know about my ability? Does he know that Emma and I are the ones who witnessed the drive-by? That we saw the driver? Was I completely surrounded this evening by the men who are responsible for Emma's attack?

Finally, Dean meets my eyes. "I told you he was a dangerous man."

"So . . . are you still . . . involved?" My heart races. Is Dean their spy? He didn't need a place to stay until shortly after Emma was attacked.

"No."

"Are you sure?" I ask without realizing it.

He shakes his head. "I'm not lying to you, Ethan."

I take a deep breath to try to calm my nerves. "How'd you get out?"

He opens his mouth to speak and then closes it again. A moment later he says, "Not right now, okay? One thing at a time. It wasn't the best time in my life. I'd rather not be up all night thinking about it."

"Oh okay. I'm sorry."

"Don't worry about it. I mean it. It's not your problem."

"Are we safe here?"

He nods. "Yeah. Nobody knows I'm here."

"Are they at your apartment?"

He nods. "It has to do with them, yeah."

"I thought you were scoping it out today?"

He nods. "I did. Still not safe there."

Again, my mind creates so many scenarios of what the rest of the story entails. He must've ditched them somehow. But these men aren't idiots. Dean didn't move that far away. Despite what he said, the Martellis must know that he's here.

The bigger question is, if Dean was out, why all of a sudden is it a problem that he's still breathing?

I disappear to the bathroom to brush my teeth and wash my face before bed. I'm hoping my evening routine will help me relax, but I'm still too wound up by the time I return.

Dean's made up his bed on the couch. I feel bad that he doesn't have a more comfortable place to sleep—especially since he told me he used to live on the streets, not to mention everything he's probably been through with the Martellis—but short of him sharing my bed, we're fresh out of options.

"I know you don't want to talk about it anymore," I say,

lingering behind the couch, "but if you were sort of involved with everything—"

"Not everything. Very basic stuff. I never wanted to be in the business. It was just the cards I was dealt at the time."

"Okay." I glance over at Cale's door. The sound of the TV is still present. "Did you work with Bello?"

He sits up and rests his muscular arms on the back of the couch. "Do you really want to know?"

I keep my eyes on Cale's door. For all I know, Dean could've done the same thing to other girls. People do stupid things when they're stuck in a bad spot.

"No," he says with a sigh. "The family did. I knew him. Called him Uncle Mike for a while, out of respect, but I never had anything to do with his side of the business."

I suck in my bottom lip and refuse to look him in the eyes. "I want to kill him."

Dean shakes his head. "Even if we do, that's not going to stop the next Emma from getting hurt, you know? The show will still go on, no matter who's the capo of Hopman."

"So how do we make sure there aren't any more Emmas?"

"I think you're fighting a losing battle, to be honest." He lies back down.

"Maybe so, but I'm equipped with something they're not expecting."

I have to focus on what I *can* do. With the suit Wes made, I'm able to control the lightning impulses better. If nothing else, I can scare people. Isn't that what the Martellis are doing? Scaring people with threats? The only difference is, I'll be doing it to protect people, not make money.

"You're going to get yourself shot if you don't run faster."

I finally look down at him. "That's what my *trainer* is supposed to be working on." I force a quick smile. "He might not have personally put her in the hospital, but it doesn't make him any less responsible. Same goes for whoever's above him."

"Rizzo."

I didn't realize he was that high up in the crime family. "The whole thing needs to go."

Fuse: Origin

He sits up again. "Let me get this straight: You think that you can personally take down the mob?"

"Well, no. I'd need help. Which is where you come in." My face flashes red again. I'm asking him to betray the people who took him in when he was at his worst. But as good as these people once were to him, they're still bad people. They still beat and rape innocent women for witnessing something they know nothing about. He's gotta see it that way too.

Dean sighs. "Not the whole mob. It's not necessary. Not really. You take out parts—from a business standpoint. Killing their leaders doesn't do much, even if you could get to them. You need to take away the way they make money without letting it be known that it was you. After that, just stand back and watch as the whole empire implodes."

Wow. He's thought about this before. "So Michael Bello, what's his deal?"

He shrugs. "I'm not positive, but from what I've heard, it was mostly human trafficking."

My eyes bulge. "Really?"

"Not like child labor, although sometimes, yes. I'm talking prostitution. Single mothers, broke college students. They start them off small, like they did me, and then . . . "

Images of women and children being abused like Emma fill my mind. I need to think of something else if I'm going to get a good night's sleep. Judging from the monster yawn he lets out, Dean clearly has had enough of this conversation too. It's well after eleven by now.

I step toward my room, pausing in the doorway. I don't know how I'm going to free my mind enough to let me slip into sleep tonight. If Dean trusts me with his secrets, I should be able to trust him with mine. Especially if he's going to help me with the Martellis. Maybe even talk to Alex or Wes about what I'm capable of so we can come up with a better plan.

That is, if Alex has had a change of heart. Maybe once this capo thing is over she'll relax. Still, it'd be a shame not to use my ability—and that awesome suit—for something useful.

I turn and face him again. "Hey, Dean?"

Chapter Fifteen

"Mmm?" he grumbles without sitting up.

"Do you have any plans tomorrow?"

"Just kicking your ass at the gym, why?"

"I want to show you something."

"What?"

"You'll see."

Yeah, I definitely think this is the right choice. I'm actually looking forward to telling him more about what I've been doing. So few people know. It'll be good to bring someone else into the mix.

———

IF THE CLINIC wasn't in the worst part of the city, Dean would've made us run here. I guess I still need to strengthen my core and build up my speed and stamina. Even with the extensive stretches he had me do, talking and running at the gym this morning proved to be impossible. It's going to be a long road. Still, it's faster than I was a month ago.

Instead, we're whizzing down Wilkinson Avenue on the back of Dean's Ducati. It's not made for two people. I thought I could ride on the back, but I discover quickly that without the anticipation of going after a rapist, I'm pretty terrified of motorcycles.

As Dean takes off from the parking garage, I nearly fall flat on my back on the pavement. Suddenly he becomes my new best friend, and I cling to him to stay on the bike. The helmet helps squash any embarrassment I have from riding bitch.

When we come to a stop behind the clinic building, I'm grateful to be standing still.

"So whatcha think?" Dean asks with a smirk. It was his idea to take the bike out. Apparently he's not a fan of the often sardine-like experience of the subway. Then again, who is?

"Ask me again when my brain catches up."

He laughs and I lead him inside.

Debbie, the receptionist, begins to tell me to take a seat and wait for the doctor, but Alex intercepts her.

"It's all right," she says. "They can come back." She leads us behind the desk into her cramped office. Folders packed with files are stacked everywhere among coffee cups and various medical equipment. "I didn't realize you two were so close."

"He's been working with me at the gym to get me in better shape."

She cocks an eyebrow. "Bigger muscles aren't going to stop a bullet."

Desperate to avoid a lecture, I ask, "Is Wes here?"

"Yeah, let me get him." She casts a suspicious look at Dean. "Where do you want to meet him?"

"Uh, downstairs. That's kind of why we're here."

She doesn't say anything, but takes a deep breath to show her disapproval.

I lead Dean down to the basement, flipping on the lights at the bottom of the stairs, and cross the room to boot up the computer.

"This is what I've been using as a safe place for my abilities, so keep it quiet." I pull the suit out of my backpack and fold it up on the table beside the computer.

He looks around and takes a seat in the computer chair beside me. "Wouldn't it be safer at your place?"

"Maybe, but Alex and Wes have been studying my condition here for a while now. They know what is and isn't normal for me."

"So this is where you go when you do all your research?"

I nod. "I was looking up stuff about crime families here when I should've just been talking to you."

Dean gives a half-hearted grin.

Wes's voice grows louder as he approaches the top of the stairs, and Dean and I sit up straighter, anticipating his entry.

"Mr. Pierce, how are you?" he asks as he descends the stairs. "Dr. Fletcher said you brought a friend."

"This is Dean."

After they shake hands and exchange pleasantries, I turn our attention to the suit.

"I brought it back. Thought maybe it'd be better than starting from scratch."

Chapter Fifteen

"Good. How are your shocks?"

"The suit is helping, but I need to use them."

Dean looks between the two of us, confused. I make a mental note to fill him in later.

"Have you found a safe place to release them? Maybe the solar plant."

I shake my head. "What if I overload the grid and black out the whole city?"

Wes picks up the suit and examines the electrodes inside. "I wouldn't worry about that. The city creates enough energy to power the whole metro area. A lot of the energy is actually sent across the state."

"Right. I'll have to give it a try." That is, if I ever stop using them to play hero. I wonder how long I can go without releasing the energy. Probably not long. Especially if I don't want to shock every person I come in contact with.

"How soon do you think you can get the new suit ready?"

He glances up at me. "Are you in a rush to use it?"

"Actually, maybe."

His brow furrows. "I'll do it as quick as I can, but I'd rather work out as many kinks as possible before I give it back to you. Everything we're doing here is unprecedented."

"Right. Okay."

Dean watches as Wes continues to eye me. "What are your intentions with this suit?"

"I…uh…nothing."

"Smooth," Dean mutters.

Wes looks at him and then back to me, still confused. "Mr. Pierce, what's going on?"

"You know what happened the first time I wore the suit?" I don't want to voice it again. Everybody knows. I don't need the looks of pity.

He nods.

"It was the Martelli family. I can't let it go."

Wes sighs and leans against the edge of the table. "You have to be careful with them. Even if I didn't think it was a smart idea last time, I understood why you had to go. But this? It seems like you're sticking your nose where it doesn't belong."

"Where it doesn't belong?" I shout. "They went after her because we saw one of their men shoot someone on the street! Both of us! They've already come after me. Remember that? Right outside. This time they got her. It's only a matter of time before I'm the target again. I just need to beat them to the punch."

Both of them are quiet. I wonder if Dean is ever going to speak up. He probably wouldn't here. That's not to say he doesn't have his opinions.

And I can tell Wes is choosing his words carefully before he speaks. "Again, it's your choice. I'm just voicing my hesitations."

I'm breathing heavily, trying to calm myself down. These people care about me. That's all Wes is saying. I need to at least hear him out.

"I appreciate your concern, but this is something I have to do. Will you help me?"

He's quiet a moment longer. "Promise me one thing."

"What's that?"

"That once you fulfill your mission, you'll be done." His eyes bore into me. "Grief and guilt can make people do stupid things. There's a fine line between justice and vengeance."

My mission? Take down the Martelli family. For now, at least. I have a chance to make a difference. To make sure this doesn't happen to any other girls. That's a job bigger than one man can do. My mission might never be fulfilled.

"Yes, I promise."

Chapter Sixteen

Monday morning. It's time for me to return to work. I don't know if I'm prepared for this. Even in our separate cubicles, Emma and I would IM each other all day, break for lunch together, walk to the subway together on our way home.

I make sure to get there early and dress better than I normally do. Again, I don't need looks of pity and people who are just fishing for information about how she's doing and what I know. They know which hospital she's at. They could visit her.

That's exactly what I did most of yesterday. Despite my protests, Dean made us go to the gym. Leg day. After that I was glad to sit in a hospital room and give Theresa and her parents a break.

Emma's condition hasn't changed much. Theresa said the doctors discussed realistic outcomes with her and her parents on Saturday. Basically, the likelihood of Emma ever being the same is slim. But we're all still hopeful. Still, I can't help but wonder if she'll ever wake up. I've never wanted so badly to be wrong.

When I arrive at my desk I see it cluttered with Post-its and scrap pieces of paper with numbers to call back and tech things to look into. With a sigh, I plop down and begin sorting through the pile. I can only imagine how many e-mails I have waiting.

The fluorescent light above me suddenly gets dimmer and I look up to see a tall, imposing man standing on the opposite side of my corner cubicle. He's wearing black-rimmed glasses and a blue suit with brown elbow pads, yet he looks to be about my age.

"Welcome back, Mr. Pierce. Can I have a word with you?"

He doesn't look familiar, but I don't dare ask who he is. Even if I think I had a perfectly good reason to stay home last week, the company leaders likely don't see it that way. And if what Emma said is true and the board is unhappy that Tranidek paid my bills, I'm already on thin ice.

"Uh, sure." I straighten my tie as I stand up, very conscious of the fact that despite my efforts to dress nicer, I'm still the subordinate.

He leads me upstairs to his office—Emma's office.

"We need to discuss your absences," he says after we're each seated. No pleasantries. Just right to the chase.

"Right, I'm sorry about that. It's just my girlfriend—Emma Landry—she's um . . . I'm sorry, what are we doing in her office?"

He pulls at the lapels of his blue blazer. "Well, if you had shown up to work last week, you would've gotten the memo. My name's Dale Duffy, and I'm the interim IT Manager while Miss Landry is out."

They already replaced her?

"Oh."

"Oh?"

"I'm sorry. I took some time to be with her after . . . " How much do they know? " . . . everything."

"I would tell you to call next time, but I don't expect there will be a next time, correct?"

I nod obediently. "Yes—no, there won't be."

"I also expect the time you missed to be made up with comp time. Whether that means coming in early or working late is up to you. Either way, we have quotas to hit, and you're holding us

Chapter Sixteen

up for this month. Turn it around by the end of next week or we'll be having an entirely different discussion."

I have options. I know I do. I don't *need* this job. I was just offered a better one. Still, the prospect of me losing this job—the only full-time job I've ever had—makes me feel like I've let everyone down by being selfish. I wasn't the one who was put in the hospital. Emma was. I had no real reason to stay home. I should've listened to Cale and Myra.

"Yes sir," I respond.

"I expect an e-mail every evening about the status of your projects. Your daily quotas must be reached as well as enough to make up for last week, understood?"

I nod again. "Yes."

"Now get back to work. There's a lot of it."

Insignificant. That's the way I feel as I walk back to my desk in shame. What's worse is I don't have any motivation to work. I contemplate Rizzoli's offer and whether it's even still an option. If he's a part of the Martelli family, I don't want to work for him, but it's hard to pass up what looks like the perfect job on paper. Dean warned me about the dangers of those men. How much of that spills over into their day-job activities?

And what about Emma? I want to believe she's going to pull through and come back to work. Things will be just like they were before, right?

That's what I tell myself to get through the day. This is all just temporary until Emma's better. Although, deep down I know that even if she does make it home, she probably won't be the same.

———

IT'S RAINING WHEN I finally call it quits for the day at seven. I've already got my alarm set for four in the morning tomorrow. Despite the amount of work that was dumped in my lap this morning, I still need to press on with my training.

Call me stupid—or paranoid of thunderstorms—but I didn't bring an umbrella with me. Instead, I hold the collar of my jacket tight against my neck and power walk in the rain. By the time I've walked two blocks, I can feel my shirt sticking to me.

Of course, the subway line that I take is delayed for "maintenance." Meaning a rat probably chewed through a line somewhere. Looks like walking is the only way to go. It makes me a bit nervous in the dark and the rain, but I've been fine on my own before. Still, I stay alert and grip my keys between my freezing fingers.

Cars whiz by me on the street, splashing water onto the sidewalk and threatening to somehow make my day even worse. That is, until a black sedan pulls up at the end of the next block.

A man in a trench coat gets out—he's got an umbrella—and opens the back door. No one comes out, and although I intend to walk on as if I don't notice it, I look inside as I approach. That's when I hear the man with the umbrella say my name.

"Ethan Pierce, there's someone who'd like to speak with you."

Ask any city dweller and they can tell you about *the look*. The scowl you give unwanted strangers who address you on the street. The one that tells them you're not in the mood to talk.

That's the look I give this guy before I keep walking.

"It's about Emma Landry," he adds.

I stop dead. I'm sure the man smiles. How does he know her name? Then again, it can't be hard to figure out that I'm dating her. If someone's watching me, they'll be able to track my frequent visits to the hospital, the friends I share with Emma, and all our social media pointing to each other.

Spinning on my heels, I walk back to the car. My hair is soaked and rainwater drips from the end of my nose. "Who is it?"

The umbrella man motions to the open door. "See for yourself."

As stupid as I know this decision is, my curiosity gets the better of me. That and the cold water dripping down my back, sending shivers throughout my body.

I slide onto the black leather seat next to a large man in a full suit. Despite dressing better for my first day back to work, I'm underdressed compared to him. Even if I was dry.

Chapter Sixteen

He extends his hand. "Ethan Pierce, so nice to have finally met you."

I try to dry off my hand before I shake his, but my navy blue slacks are soaked. "Hi."

He doesn't offer anything else, only watches out the window as the driver directs the car through the city.

"Do you know who I am?" he asks a few minutes later.

I shake my head.

"My name's Carlo Martelli. I'm sure you've heard of me."

My heart stops cold, and it takes all I have not to look surprised. Still, I have to drop my hands to my knees to keep them from shaking.

Carlo Martelli came up in nearly every article I read about the Martelli family. Racketeering, conspiracy, tax evasion—these are just some of the cases brought against him throughout his life. Somehow, he's always managed to slip through.

"You've certainly made quite the name for yourself, haven't you? The boy—I'm sorry—the *man* who was struck by lightning and survived."

Is this it? Did I just make the same mistake Emma did before she was jumped? Am I going to die tonight? Worse?

He flashes me a set of white teeth. Between them and his silver hair, his olive skin is even more noticeable. "Relax. I'm not going to hurt you. Why would I do that when I personally asked Frank Rizzoli to make sure you had a job?"

"You asked him to give me a job?"

Another chuckle. "Yes, I did."

The thought of working for the family who put Emma in the hospital—among whatever other corruption they're spreading throughout the city—sickens me. And I had dinner with both Rizzoli *and* Bello. I'm a lot closer to the Martellis than I'd like to be.

"What do you want?" I barely recognize my voice. It's a croak, a whisper. I left my strength back on the street.

"You're a hard man to track down. I admire that. I mean, we've found your apartment, your place of work, but you never seem to stick around at one place for long. And like I said, I don't want to hurt you. Or scare you."

Scaring me is exactly what he's doing. He found my apartment. Does that mean he knows about Dean? Does he care? What about Cale? Is he in danger now too?

I swallow hard, keeping my hands firmly on my knees. "So what do you want?"

"I understand you witnessed something very tragic a couple weeks ago."

"Murder." There it is! My voice is back with more conviction, even a little bite.

"If you knew the man, you would not have so much sympathy for him. Men like him are the reason Olympia is in such bad shape. Hopman specifically. What do you know about that man, Mr. Pierce?"

I shake my head. "Nothing, really."

"His legal name was Carlos Wilson. His street name was One Shot. He was a gang leader and drug dealer. My men in Hopman have been clearing out his gang for the last several months. I'm sure you noticed he was alone that night."

"A few homeless men were with him."

Martello grins. "Loyal customers, I'm sure. Gangs and drugs— they're horrible. Completely unacceptable, in my opinion, and yet that wasn't even his worst crime. He needed to be taken care of."

"You mean killed."

He shrugs. "It's unfortunate when these things happen, but I can't argue with its effectiveness. Certainly sends a message."

"Murder is bad, but rape is okay?" That slipped out by accident, but I'm happy that I've finally caught him off guard.

His smile fades. "No. Absolutely not. Wilson was a disgrace to men everywhere with his prostitution circles."

"What about my friend?"

He nods slowly. "Ah, that's what's been on your mind. What happened to Miss Landry is unfortunate, and I can assure you that the men who did that to her will be taken care of. The order was never to harm her. Only to convince her not to talk about that night. I will personally see to it that those men never touch another woman."

Chapter Sixteen

I don't know whether I can believe him. From the research I've done, rape has never been among the list of crimes committed by the Martellis. They have a higher—although warped—sense of morality than that. But Emma is still in the hospital, and Aiden Lipinski said Michael Bello gave the orders. Was Lipinski lying?

After I killed one of the Martelli men, Emma was the easy target. Someone who would scare easy and convince me not to say anything. Someone who wouldn't fight back.

The thought occurs to me that I could kill Carlo Martelli right here. My fingers buzz with excess energy, so much so that if he touched me, I'd probably shock him without even trying. If I concentrate enough, I could do it.

"Why are you telling me all this?" I ask.

"It was my original intension to make sure you were silenced. You saw one of my men and had to be taken care of. Which is why I sent Mr. Lacey after you."

"The man who tried to murder me?"

He grins. "The man you managed to kill without touching a single weapon."

I stare at him wordlessly. How much does he know about Lacey's death? Did anyone see us? We were standing on the street, so it's possible, but the police said there were no witnesses.

I swallow. "So what does that mean?"

"I admire your determination. In my younger years, I was given the nickname the Invincible Man. After Lacey's death, I saw a bit of myself in you."

"Are you trying to recruit me?"

He smiles at me. "Not at the moment. No, I wanted to speak with you to personally apologize for the actions of the men who harmed your friend. As a favor to you, they will be taken care of." He taps the seat beside my leg. "But in the meantime, I'll need a favor from you."

"What's that?" I ask carefully. He may not hurt me right now, but he could later. He knows where I spend my time. Worse, he could go after someone else I care about. My mind wanders to Cale, Myra, and my parents. Does he have men waiting to hurt them if I don't agree to help him?

"Bear in mind, what I'm about to propose goes against my usual instincts, but as I've said, I see a little of me in you."

"What is it?" The anticipation is killing me.

"I'll keep you and your loved ones safe if you don't breathe a word about anything related to my family's operations."

I lick my cracked lips. "I've already talked to the police about that night."

He waves this off. "From here on out."

I nod. "Okay." There's nothing left to tell. Not to the police anyway. And I have no intention of telling Cale or my parents just how close I've come to the Martellis. They would really have me locked up then.

He calls up to the driver. "Right here's fine."

The car pulls over to the curb. I have no idea what part of the city we're in. I haven't been paying attention, and the tinted windows in the rain obstruct the views outside.

"Oh, and one more thing."

I take a deep breath. I thought I was free.

"You accept Mr. Rizzoli's offer to work for Tranidek."

He wants to keep an eye on me. He wants to make sure I'm not talking to anyone about their family. He wants to bribe me with a cushy job so I don't talk.

"I'll have to think about it." I turn to exit, but he grabs my arm.

"You'll do more than think about it."

Our eyes lock and I can see the man's vindictive determination. The chills I get have nothing to do with the rain or the cold.

Finally, he lets me go. "I wish you well, Mr. Pierce. Thank you for your time."

The car door opens, and the man with the umbrella hooks his hand under my arm and pulls me out of the car. Standing in the pouring rain on a dark residential street, I watch as the black sedan pulls away.

Did I just seal my fate? Did I just get in bed with the Martelli family? What does that mean for my family?

Cale would kill me if I called him to pick me up. My mind is

Chapter Sixteen

replaying the conversation Martelli, and I can't think of a plausible excuse for me to be out here.

I walk to a street corner to figure out where I am—Benjamin Street and West Carolina Boulevard—before I call Dean to pick me up. He doesn't ask questions, just says he'll be there. I'm very thankful for him in Emma's absence. He's been a good friend, which is exactly what I need.

The parkways on the west side of the city are beautiful, even in the rain. I follow along Flint Parkway to where North and South Main Streets merge into one. Hopefully Dean will be able to see me better from here. It's the Midtown Theatre District, and the glow of the lights makes me feel safer, if nothing else.

As I walk, I consider what Martelli said. Could I work at Tranidek knowing I'd be under the watchful eye of the Martellis? Will he hold up his promise to keep me and the people I care about safe if I don't immediately call Rizzoli?

Dean has pulled up on the corner of Main Street with his bike by time I make it there. He's got a leather jacket and a spare helmet in a bag on his back. I'm grateful because I know the wind would tear through me with my sopping clothes.

I take a long hot shower as soon as I get home. Dean doesn't ask any questions, though I know he has a million of them. By the time I get out, I see he's been working in the kitchen.

I call Cale to check in with him and make sure he's okay. I breathe a sigh of relief when he tells me he just got back to Myra's apartment and is staying there for the night. She lives two blocks from the library downtown, and he was probably doing more research into the Works.

My parents are next on the list to call. They're both safe, but the phone call seems to drag on as they pester me with questions about how I'm feeling after the lightning strike, how Emma's doing, how I'm holding up with it all. Mom even suggests I go see a psychiatrist. As if I have time for that with all the work I need to make up at the office.

Dean doesn't ask questions as we eat. Only the sound of our silverware clinking against our plates fills the room. He seems preoccupied with something himself, but I don't push it. It's not until he takes his plate to the sink that he finally speaks up.

"What were you doing in Midtown?"

"It's a long story."

"I have all night."

"Not now, Dean. It's been a long day."

He sighs. "Ethan, you're dealing with very powerful people. I need to know something. I don't want anything bad to happen to you." He looks like he's going to say something else but doesn't.

"It has to do with the Martellis."

"Did they hurt you?"

I place my plate in the sink on top of his. "No, nothing like that. Look, I'm tired and I just want to pass out. I'll tell you later, but for now you just need to trust me, okay?"

He nods and heads to the bathroom to brush his teeth.

I'll tell him tomorrow. He's right. It's probably best that *someone* knows what I'm dealing with, but I'm still processing it all. What I need most right now, though, is a good night's sleep.

With my belly full, I crawl into bed and immediately pass out. The cold and the long hours have drained me of all my energy.

CHAPTER SEVENTEEN

If my extended work hours aren't enough to tire me out, Dean's intensified training is. Each day builds off the previous day. Monday he let me go easy with a simple three-mile run before work. Well, he called it simple. I called it hell. He claims I'm going to be able to run five miles by Christmas. Ha!

After work on Tuesday we did a two-mile run and almost an hour of weight training. Yesterday morning before work, the two-mile run and beginner's boxing lessons nearly killed me. I went straight to bed after dinner last night. The meals Dean's been preparing have been heartier. A lot more food than I'm used to eating, but with the training regimen Dean has us doing, I need it.

Dean woke me up early this morning for another run. In the rain. I had a few choice words for him as I got myself ready for our workout.

It's been a few days since I met with Carlo Martelli, but my fears still plague me. The news yesterday morning proved that he follows through on his promises. Aiden Lipinski and George Kingston's bodies were found at the rocky bottom of Emerson

Bluffs, charred and dismembered. Their dental records were the only thing that identified them.

As relieved as I am that Emma's abusers got what was coming to them, I'm terrified by the severity of the attack. Those men weren't just murdered, they were mutilated. What does that mean if I piss off the wrong people, which could very well happen if I don't accept Rizzoli's offer?

I thought that with all the work I'm doing at the gym and at the office that I'd be sleeping well, but almost every night I wake up in a cold sweat after a recurring nightmare. Carlo Martelli executing each person I care about. Dean even made it into the dream last night, but that might've been because he woke up and asked if I was okay.

Surprisingly, though, my run each each energizes me. It's amazing to discover how much you're really out of shape until you start to push yourself out of your comfort zone. What's even more amazing is when you notice your improvement. I finish our two miles tired, but with noticeably more energy.

"You feeling good?" Dean asks as we head into the gym. He planned our route to end up here. Granted, it's only two blocks from my apartment, but I certainly wasn't paying attention to where we were going.

I grumble in response. I should've known the run wasn't the whole workout.

Inside, we head to the second floor to a large room they use for different classes. Zumba, pilates, yoga, the occasional pizza night. Dean pulls out several mats from the stack in the corner and lays them on the floor so there's a large square in the center.

"Okay," he says clapping his hands together. "Ready?"

He doesn't have the punch pads like he did the other day for the boxing lesson. Instead, he's crouching down just a little and inching closer to me, bouncing back and forth.

"What are you doing?"

"Come on." He reaches for my arm, but I swat him away and take a step back.

"What's going on?"

Chapter Seventeen

Standing up straighter, he says, "You wanna learn to fight, right?"

I shrug. "Well, yeah."

He raises his hand and counts off on his fingers. "Running will help get you in shape faster. Weight lifting will build your strength. Boxing will teach you how to punch and defend at a close distance." He drops his hand and points to the mat. "Wrestling will help increase your endurance."

What was I saying about my comfort zone? Wrestling just seems . . . awkward. I haven't wrestled since Cale and I were in high school. He was on the wrestling team and loved that he could easily overpower me.

Dean shows me how to start, making sure I keep my body loose and ready, but the first time around he still manages to pin me.

"These men you're going after, they don't play nice," he says as I lay flat on the mat. "I'm talking nut shots, eye gouging, anything. If you're down, they'll keep kicking until you're dead." He offers his hand and helps me up. We go again.

Another lunge at me, and I'm back on the floor, half on top of him as he wraps his arm under one of mine and reaches across my body to pin my other one. He lets me go and pops to his feet, offering his hand again.

"You're bigger than me. That's not fair." I know I'm whining and making excuses, but I don't know how I'm going to take down someone his size. At least, not without zapping them.

"It's not going to be fair. And size isn't as big of an issue as you'd think. You can do it. Come on, let's go again."

We work at it for half an hour, making the most of the little time I have in the morning before work. I'm sweaty and tired and have successfully pinned him at least once this morning. Dean's happy with my progress, but I still think everything's going too slow. I'm not going to be ready in time.

———

FUSE: ORIGIN

WITH MY WORKWEEK spent staying late at the office and training with Dean in my spare time, today's the first day I can meet with Myra for lunch. I came in an hour early to work after Dean and I finished up at the gym, and since city hall is only two blocks from my office, meeting for lunch worked out perfect.

Now that I know that the Hopman capo is none other than Michael Bello, I need to dig around to see if there's any dirt on him. More than what can be printed in the paper. I don't have to follow the same procedures law enforcement does. If Myra heard a rumor, I can look into it.

Cale doesn't know anything more than what's on the news. I grilled him last night at dinner. I figured he's been keeping up-to-date with the latest development sites in the city, but I guess I have the wrong developer. If I needed dirt on Leon Wallace, Cale would probably have a whole slew of new rumors on him.

"Gosh, I've been so busy this past week that I've barely had time to myself," she says as she takes a seat across from me at the Buzzing Bar on the first floor of my building.

"Yeah, I've noticed Cale's been staying at your place more this week." Which usually means nighttime is the only time they can see each other.

She unwraps her sandwich. "He's busy with his research and I've . . . " She takes a bite into her sandwich, apparently not willing to divulge in what she's been working on.

"Oh, I get it. They've replaced Emma already at work—"

"What!"

"Temporarily, but still. Anyway, this new guy is kind of an ass. Says I need to make up for the time I took off."

She rocks her head a bit as she chews. "Well, your brother and I both told you—"

"It was bereavement. It doesn't matter anyway. I should be able to catch up on everything so I can go back to my regular schedule."

"That's good. You look exhausted."

I roll my eyes. "Thanks."

"You know what I mean. I'm sure I've looked better too."

I swallow the bite I took and continue, "You look great. But

Chapter Seventeen

yeah, I've been going to the gym a lot too."

Despite feeling like my muscles are turning to soup and the routine ass-kicking from Dean killing my ego, I'm happy with the changes I've already started to see in my body. My face looks slimmer, and Dean says the strength of my heart is probably back up to where it was before the strike.

"Yeah, Cale told me about that." She takes a sip of her bottled water. "I think it's great. Everyone needs to take care of themselves. I haven't been able to get to the gym this week as often as I usually do, but I definitely want to get back to it. Where do you go?"

"Oh, just some place near my apartment. It's kind of small compared to the big gyms."

"I come over here." She points behind her and across the street. The Grid Mall has two of the chain gyms.

"So what have you been so busy with at work?" I take a bite of the second half of my sandwich, hoping my silence will force her to continue talking.

"Just legal stuff, mostly."

"Legal stuff?" I mumble around my food.

"Yeah. I'm not a lawyer, so reading through some of these official documents is confusing. I have to keep looking stuff up, and it's taking me awhile."

"Anything interesting?"

She smiles over her water bottle. "You know I can't tell you that."

Just as I thought. She's tight-lipped. Still, I wonder if I can tap into her empathy for me.

"Does it have anything to with the Martellis?"

"What makes you say that?"

"I've been doing some research myself."

She rolls her head back and groans. "Ethan, please be careful with that. You don't know who's involved. Word can spread quickly that someone is poking their nose into things they shouldn't be."

If only she knew that I met the crime boss himself. I haven't even told Dean the whole story. He's going to freak out, and I want an action plan in mind before he does.

I don't say anything to her comment. With another precious minute passing, I change tactics.

"I had dinner with the president of Tranidek last weekend."

"Oh yeah! How was that?"

"Um . . . fancy."

She laughs because she knows me. "Not a fan of rubbing elbows with the rich and famous?"

"Uh, no." I smile. "Not all of us can work for a city councilman."

She doesn't say anything, but I notice her mouth tighten a bit.

"What?"

"Nothing." The paper her sub was wrapped in now sits in a ball in front of her. "It's a great job, just not all that glamorous."

"True, but you get all the inside info on everything happening in the city."

"Never meet your idols, though."

I narrow my eyes, forgetting about fishing for information on Bello. "Are you okay? I thought you loved working for Mr. Lloyd."

She sighs. "I wanted this job so I could help the city. I wanted to make big changes, like fixing up blighted neighborhoods, removing the Manhattan Expressway, creating opportunities for small businesses to start and thrive. But . . . "

"But the job's not all you thought it'd be?"

She shakes her head. "It's not that. Not really. I knew there'd be a lot of paperwork and political stuff, but I didn't realize there was this much corruption."

My ears perk up, and I'm sure she notices the change in my demeanor. "Corruption? Like who?"

"Nothing." Yup, she definitely noticed. "I've said too much." She squeezes her trash in her fist and makes to get up, but I stop her.

"Myra, you just told me that I need to be careful with what I'm looking into. I'm just a witness to a crime. You're a city councilman's assistant. You know some of these people, don't you?"

CHAPTER SEVENTEEN

Sucking in her bottom lip, she nods.

"Who is it? Is it Mr. Lloyd?"

"Promise you won't say anything," she says as an admission. "I can't prove it yet, but I have strong suspicions that he's the one blocking improvement projects in Hopman."

So Frank Lloyd has his own agenda. A big city councilman with some hidden motives? Oh, how surprising.

"Is he the only one?"

She gives in and says, "He's the highest up that I know of, yes, but there are others, I'm sure. All throughout city government."

Still not surprised.

"Please be careful."

She shoots me a look. "You do the same."

"Deal."

————

"SO THAT WAS a bust?" Dean asks after work.

I'm sitting at the counter, watching him make dinner. He doesn't make it every day, but he does it often enough that he knows where everything is now without asking. Cale texted me to say he's staying at Myra's again tonight, so I would've been on my own for dinner anyway.

"I mean, not a total bust," I respond. "It was a nice lunch, and I got some gossip about our city leaders."

Dean eyes me from the stove. "Yeah, well, a nice lunch and some gossip is not going to bring down Bello."

The steak sizzles on the pan. Since I'm the one who usually does the grocery shopping, I know for a fact that we didn't have any in the house. He must've picked some up while I was at work.

"Well, that's not entirely true. Having lunch with Myra not only was seeing my brother's girlfriend for a midday meal, but it also continued my relationship with a city councilman's assistant. Someone with inside knowledge."

He pulls a pan out of the oven and the scent of garlic fills the room. He grabs something from the fridge and sprinkles it over the pan.

FUSE: ORIGIN

"Anyway," I continue, "she also told me that there are plenty of people in the city government who are corrupt."

He pulls two plates out of the cupboard. "I know."

His certainty startles me. "You know?"

"Back in my day I saw some of Olympia's finest acting pretty chummy with some of Olympia's most untouchable men. I can't imagine that's changed much. Especially now that some money is coming back into Olympia."

"True."

He sets a plate in front of me and walks around to take the seat to my right. I look down. A small piece of meat is sitting in the corner of the plate, and the rest is filled with oven-roasted broccoli. My stomach grumbles in response. I just ate a couple hours ago, but I'm hungry again.

"So how is the corruption going to help us?" he asks. "We're going after a man who we know is dangerous but nobody else does."

I cut into my steak and take a bite. I'm not a huge fan of red meat, but I was raised never to complain about a free meal. Besides, my first bite leaves me wanting more.

"This is all speculation, so bear with me."

He seems to roll his eyes, but I ignore him.

"Myra kept saying that she's been doing her own research. From what I guess, it's on the corruption of the city leaders."

"Why would she do that? That would piss off the rest of the people on the council and would get her fired." He points to my plate. "Eat it before it gets cold."

I reluctantly try the broccoli. Childhood flashbacks of sitting at the dinner table alone with a plate full of broccoli flashes in my mind. Surprisingly, this doesn't taste half bad. With each bite I take, I actually start to like it.

"Maybe," I say, "but Myra doesn't necessarily care about that. She wanted to work for the city to change things and help people. Doing the right thing is her first priority."

"So she's going to get herself fired to help people?"

I let out a deep breath. Frustration builds with each new interruption. "I don't know. What I'm saying is, she's looking into

Chapter Seventeen

the city's corruption. Sooner or later, she's going to expose them for what they are. We just need to link Bello to that."

Dean shakes his head. "I don't think it's going to work." He shovels the last of his food into his mouth.

"Why not?"

"If the police and the media and everyone are focused on the rogue councilman, nobody's going to care about a property developer's scandal."

He's right. Bello's involvement with the Martellis wouldn't be front page news if the story of the councilman's corruption breaks at the same time. But we still need to frame him somehow.

"So what do you suggest we do?" I ask.

I watch as he rinses his plate in the sink. The muscles in his arms shift with each movement. Finally, he leans against the counter as he dries his hands with a dish towel.

"I may have an idea, but it's risky."

I narrow my eyes. "What is it?"

"One of the biggest rules in organized crime is not to write anything down, so there are no records to find anywhere of anyone's involvement. But the family is involved in a lot of businesses involving a lot of people. We'll just need to find a witness who's willing to point to Bello doing something wrong. Actually, we'll need several witnesses."

"And I take it you can help find some of these people?"

He nods. "Yeah, but you're going to need to wear the suit to talk to them. If they're fessing up, they're going to take down everyone they can. Including me."

I try not to look so worried. "You think they'd be able to put you away if you were named?"

"Probably. The major players in the family have avoided arrest for so long, they'll take anyone they can get."

I nod and scoop up the last bit of my food.

"So we're looking for the people involved in his human trafficking?"

"Well, the people who are still involved will be loyal to him. We'll have to go back further. There are a couple people I'm

Fuse: Origin

thinking of who may even be able to help your brother's girl-friend expose Frank Lloyd, too."

"How so?"

He flashes a smile. "That's what Olympia's vigilante will have to find out."

CHAPTER EIGHTEEN

Wes really stepped it up with the new suit. It still has the same lightning bolt from my right arm to my heart, but now I've got a fresh pair of boots that are comfortable enough to run in while still providing a solid enough base for any surface. I've also got a face mask, which is surprisingly breathable, and my hands don't sweat in the new gloves, either. From head to toe, I'm covered.

The best improvement by far is the addition of the radio that fits in my right ear—or "com," as Wes calls it. With it, someone can be off-site backing me up with further intel if I need it.

Even though it's late, I know Myra will still be here. She's a key piece to incriminating both Michael Bello and Frank Lloyd. She just can't know that Ethan Pierce is involved. Which is why Fuse is the one sneaking into Myra's office so late at night.

Her desk lamp is the only one on. She has a small office next to Lloyd's. The outer room has several desks and cubicles, almost like my office. Except that city hall was built in the early 1900s, when architecture was still important. I work in a box.

I don't want to scare her, but I know that's exactly what I'll do. The black suit keeps me hidden in the shadows as I creep closer to her office. Looking through the window of the door, I see she's got her head deep in some paperwork. Folders and other files are spread across her desk.

Nervously, I knock, which makes her jump. She screams when she sees me and almost falls backward in her chair.

I clear my throat, trying to disguise my voice.

"I'm not going to hurt you," I say softly.

"I don't have anything!" she shouts, jumping to her feet.

"I need your help."

With heavy breaths, she stops and stares at me. Her eyes flicker across her desk, likely looking for a weapon.

"With what?" she asks.

"Greg Griswold."

"What about him?"

"I need his current address."

She relaxes a little. "What is this, a joke? I don't even know who that is."

"You work with Frank Lloyd, right?"

"What is this about?"

"Your boss and Greg Griswold worked together at Montgomery Works before it moved out of the city."

"So what?"

"So I need you to find his address!" I shout. Maybe a little fear will make her move quicker. There has to be a security guard downstairs. I managed to get in through a side entrance I found in a blueprint.

"How am I supposed to have his address?"

"Your boss might."

She nods and slinks back down to her seat. "Okay. I'll have to look it up in the directory. It's going to be a minute."

"Hurry." I see her reach for her phone and add, "Don't call the police until I leave."

Taking a deep breath, Myra punches her keyboard a few times with her fingers and scrolls through.

Greg Griswold is someone Dean thinks would be willing to testify against the Martellis and those involved with them. He

Chapter Eighteen

was the president of Montgomery Works until a side deal of his with the Martellis got busted. Once it became front page news, they turned on him.

When Carlo Martelli took over as the boss, he spared Griswold. But his reputation was destroyed. Worse, the Martellis were actively silencing him, targeting any reporter who covered stories about him and threatening his family. Essentially, Greg Griswold faded from the public's memory.

"The most recent address I can find is 110 Concord Street," Myra says, breaking into my thoughts.

"When was it last updated?"

She eyes me suspiciously, then glances at her computer. "Uh, looks like five years ago."

"Thank you," I say and turn to leave. Sirens blare and an alarm sounds. She must've dialed 911 or something without me looking.

Shit.

I break out in a sprint, heading for a window I know looks out onto the roof of a lower level. Zapping the glass before I get there, I jump through without hesitation. Only, the roof below is farther down than I thought. Two stories.

Crashing down, I do a quick check of my body to make sure nothing's broken. Sore as hell, but I'm all intact.

I break into a nearby window, which sets off another alarm, and sprint toward the fire exit. By the time I get to the ground floor, sirens fill the air. I spot a police car with its doors open and no one inside. I shoot a string of lightning at it, and it bursts into flames.

As the police clamor to it, I take off in the opposite direction and lose myself in the shadows of the city.

———

EVEN THOUGH MOST of the city's housing is row houses, Greg Griswold lives in a part of the city that was redeveloped in the late '60s to attract suburbanites. It worked, and people flocked to the newly developed houses. Over the last sixty years, the population has aged, and the area now contains a significant percentage of the city's seniors.

"Odd place to find a former criminal," I say into my com.

"After he was fired, the Martellis cut off all his accounts," Dean tells me from back at the clinic. "Must've had to move back in with his mother."

I'm standing under a tree on the opposite side of the street. The cloudy sky and the flickering streetlight give me enough cover in the darkness.

"She's going to have a heart attack if she sees me."

"Are there any lights on?" he asks.

"No."

"Wonder if he's got a basement bedroom, then."

"Sad life," I say before sprinting across the street.

Only one car is in the driveway, but there is a side door that's unlocked. It squeaks when I open it, and I freeze when I see a light on in the house. The intermittent sound of a TV carries up from the basement. I leave the door open in case I need to make a quick escape and slowly go downstairs, hoping the stairs won't creak.

I don't really have a solid plan. Back at city hall I just needed Myra to do one thing for me. Scaring her worked for that. But I need to have a conversation with Griswold. I need to get his testimony on record.

The bedroom to the right of the stairs where the light is coming from is empty. The TV in the corner is playing the late night news. A couple of the frames on the wall hold degrees from Olympia University.

Actually, there isn't much in the room at all. A bed, a dresser, a bookshelf, and a couple pictures—

"Who the hell are you?"

Spinning around, I realize I've let my guard down. I'm lucky I don't have a bullet in my back. Nope, the way the man's eyes flicker to the bookshelf at my right, that's where his gun is.

"I'm here to talk about what happened with you, Michael Bello, and Frank Lloyd." I try to make my voice as deep as I can get it. It sounds forced, but it's the best I can do.

Chapter Eighteen

"What is this, Halloween? What the hell are you wearing? Get out of my house!"

"I'm working on a case that will bring down Bello and Lloyd for the criminals that they are."

He shrugs. "Okay, I'll humor you. You think you can take down those men? Take it from a guy who tried. You can't."

"I have connections."

"They'll destroy you."

"They don't know me," I counter.

"You think hiding behind some mask is going to save you from them? Wrong, kid. They'll figure out who you are, where you live, where you work, and piece by piece they'll take away everything you have until you break."

Images of Emma flash in my head. They've already started. Who are they going to target next?

"If you've already lost everything, what more do you have to lose?"

He chews on the inside of his lip and lets out a huff of air. "What do you need?"

"Your testimony. There will be others, but the more detailed you are the better."

"That's not going to do shit. It's been too long. It'll be my word against theirs."

Electricity sparks between my fingers. "If you want to spend the rest of your life wallowing in your pity, then so be it. But I'm going to try to put a stop to that family taking advantage of this city."

I take a step toward him to exit, but he puts up his hand.

"What makes you think you have a chance of bringing these guys down?" he asks.

"I told you, I have connections."

"Who are they?"

"They're at city hall." There's no way I'd ever give up Myra's name.

"And they have a case against these men already?"

The mask hides the apprehension on my face. I know Myra's gathering evidence against Lloyd, but what about Bello? Other than Dean's word about his shady dealings, I have nothing. Dean wouldn't ever let me use his testimony, so I'm relying on Griswold's and others.

"Yes," I lie.

"Take off the mask."

"No."

"How do I know I can trust you? How do I know you're not some reporter?"

"I'm not." Another surge of lightning crackles between my fingers as I glare at him. Finally, I step toward the exit and say, "I'll find someone else."

"Wait." He closes his eyes and pauses. "I'll help."

Stepping back a comfortable distance, I cross my arms and wait for him to continue.

"You gonna get something out to record?"

"Just talk." Dean is recording this conversation back at the clinic. I add as an afterthought, "State your name first, though."

He sighs. "Gregory Griswold."

"Thank you. Go on."

"Okay, the whole thing was kind of sketchy," he starts. "Looking back, right from the beginning it was weird. Frank Lloyd had been a good friend of mine. We lived down the street from each other when I bought my place on Broadway."

He moves and takes a seat on the bed.

"At the time, I had been working for the city at the water and sewer plant on the waterfront. Just a laborer, but it paid well. By then, the city had started to go down and they needed to let some people go. I was one of them. When Frank heard, he mentioned that he might have a position for me."

"What did Frank do?"

"He worked at Montgomery. Said he was good friends with the owner, that he was looking to step back a bit and needed someone to fill in. I thought that someone was Frank and I'd be taking his job."

"That's when you became president?"

He nods. "Barely even had an interview. Frank and I chatted at a bar one weekend, and the following Monday I got the offer letter in the mail."

Chapter Eighteen

"What about Michael Bello?"

"Didn't know him at the time. He was just one of the investors in the company. Didn't meet him until a Christmas party a few years after I started working there. That's when he told me he was looking to make some money on the side."

"What kind of money?"

"An underground casino. That was, uh, full-service." He rubs the stubble on his chin. "Drinks, drugs, cards, *girls*."

I nod and try not to react. Looks like Bello's trafficking days started a long time ago.

"Thought he could use part of Montgomery's warehouse space for it. Private entrance in an industrial area next to the airport, so noise wasn't ever an issue. Paid me a quarter of the profits each week for it." He grins. "Money, man. Lots of it. Bought a penthouse in Midtown—this was back before your time, when Lakeside Village was still trash."

"What about the police?"

He shrugs. "Bello and Lloyd said they knew a few of the cops and they were cool. I didn't ask questions. My guess is they were paying them off."

"So what happened?"

"Things were good for a couple years. The few times I visited, it seemed like the city's most elite citizens were always there. Mayor Banks, even. Then things got bad."

"How?"

"I was working late one night. I could hear the muffles of the music playing, but then it got quiet. Real quiet. Next thing I know, I'm hearing gunshots and screams. I run over there, but most of the crowd had cleared out by then." He shakes his head again. "The police came and assumed it was me who organized it all. I was the president. I was working late. Hell, I even heard the music before the gunshots. The cop who took me in was probably the guy they were paying off.

"I was arrested and spent a night in jail. Mikey came to visit. Only he wanted to make sure I wouldn't say anything. Said they would get me out if I got put away for it. So I kept my mouth shut."

He shakes his head. "Should've just told the truth. The police didn't have enough evidence to convict me, so I was a freed man. But now Mikey needed to find a new place for the casino."

"So where did you run into trouble?" I ask.

"About two months after my trial. Frank Lloyd had been on different boards for the city and was working his way up to an elected office. He came to Montgomery representing some permit board for the city and claimed it failed to pass the environmental review since we were handling toxic chemicals."

"I thought Montgomery moved to Terry Lake because business had died off?"

"Oh, it *did*. People began doing business elsewhere after the scandal with the casino and my trial. But that's not the way the story was being told. Suddenly, my arrest and the casino slipped off the news' radar and the new story was that I was doing such a horrible job as president.

"I was let go, that facility was shut down and moved out of the city, and no reporter would even give me the time of day. I went to Frank, I went to Mikey, and both of them said I had nothing to worry about. Then the death threats came.

"My accounts were frozen. Sold my penthouse to hide, but they found me. They smashed my car, robbed my place of everything worth anything. I honestly thought it was only a matter of time before I was at the bottom of the lake."

"So . . . ?" I press.

"I think I scared them. They didn't think I'd stay quiet, so they wanted to make sure I did. Not only that, but the rest of the family started acting differently. Frank and Mikey both got real jobs, distancing themselves from the Martellis. It wasn't until Sal died that the harassment stopped."

"Who replaced him?"

"Carlo Martelli. Once he took over, the attention shifted. The family laid low for a little while, tried to get their names out of the papers. I'm sure they weren't completely innocent during that time."

"What about the threats?"

"Carlo said I was a freed man. He wanted a clean slate to

Chapter Eighteen

make up for the bridge Sal burned during his time. But my windows still get smashed, tires slashed, and not very many people in the city are willing to hire me anymore."

"If Carlo gave you a pass, who's targeting you?"

He shrugs. "I can't be sure, but my guess would be Bello and Lloyd. They both have high profiles now. Especially Lloyd. If word got out that he was actually the one in charge of that underground casino, I'd be dead so fast I wouldn't know it was coming."

"So you gave up?"

"What would you do if you were me?" he shouts. "Of course I gave up! You can't fight them."

"So why tell me?" I ask for my own curiosity. "If the Martellis have you so scared, why tell your story to a stranger in a mask?"

"You've got enough," Dean mutters through the com.

"I saw the reports of you on the news. The one who could shoot lightning from his hands. Thought it was impossible and started looking into you. You were there when that girl got raped, and then her abusers ended up at the bottom of Emerson Bluffs. Seemed to me like you took care of that pretty quickly. I only hope you do the same this time around."

"Thank you, Mr. Griswold."

CHAPTER NINETEEN

"When do you think it'll be safe to go back to your place?" I ask as we head up the stairs to my apartment the next day.

Dean shrugs. "I could scope it out again. I don't want to show up too often, because there might be someone lingering."

"Do you know who it is?" Maybe I can play vigilante again and scare away whoever's bothering his apartment. He checked it out last week and said it wasn't safe, but I wonder if that's changed.

"I have an idea," he says.

I'm about to ask for more details, but we reach my floor.

"Hey, there you are." Cale's finishing off a piece of pizza over the sink when we walk in. The empty box sitting on the counter will likely stay there all night.

"Yeah, we just went to the gym." I toss my bag just inside my room and take a seat at the counter. I tell Dean, "You can get in the shower first."

Myra almost runs into Dean when he heads to the

Chapter Nineteen

bathroom. "Whoops, sorry about that." A moment later, the door closes.

Cale points to it and asks, "When's his place going to be ready?"

"I don't know."

"Who is he?" Myra asks.

"Ethan's gym buddy," Cale says in a mocking tone.

"Anyway," I roll my eyes, "what are you guys up to tonight?"

"I am swamped with work," Myra says. "I found a very convenient piece of evidence on my desk this morning." She eyes me suspiciously.

"Who sent it?" I play dumb. I snuck in first thing this morning and dropped it off after Dean found another witness for me to get a testimony from.

She shrugs. "I don't know. But I have to authenticate it before I can really do anything with it . . . which is going to take some time."

Cale crosses his arms. "Try not to stay too late. I don't like knowing that that creep in a body suit cornered you yesterday."

"He came to your office last night?" I ask incredulously. I steal a look at Cale, who doesn't react to my faked surprise.

She stuffs her papers in her briefcase. "Yeah. I'll be fine. A security guard will be watching my floor specifically. Plus, the window repairmen will probably be in there. They usually work outside of regular office hours."

He leans in and gives her a kiss before she leaves. Shaking his head, he says, "I love her drive, but she really does work too much sometimes."

"Yeah. So are you in for the night, then?"

"I've got nothing better to do." Cale moves to the couch and turns on the TV. "What about you?"

"Not much. Just probably heading to bed. I'm still working overtime, so I'll be up early tomorrow, too."

"That new boss still riding your ass?"

"Yeah. He seems to keep piling on the work. I don't know

if I'll be able to finish." My daily responsibilities seem to have grown since Mr. Duffy took Emma's job. It's almost like he wants me to quit.

"That sucks, man. But I can see it his way. You didn't call in or anything."

"Yeah." It's all I have to say on the subject. I get it. I messed up and now I'm paying the consequences.

"Myra and I went to see Emma the other day. She's, uh . . . "

My chest tightens. "Yeah. She's still hanging in there."

What a line. I haven't been down to see her as much as I should. I guess I'm still not okay with seeing her as a victim. And I hate myself for that. She'd be mad at me if she knew that I was feeling sorry for her, but how am I supposed to feel?

I guess that's the point. My feelings on the subject don't make a damn bit of difference. She *is* the victim. It happened to *her*, not me. Still, I care a lot about her. I hate to see her like this.

"You're not still going down to that clinic, are you?"

"No." It comes out easier than I expect. All this lying is new. Cale and I used to be so close, even if he did have a superior attitude on occasion. But he's my big brother; it's ingrained in him. Since the lightning storm, things have changed. There are so many new aspects of my life, and I haven't included him in many of them.

Cale and Dean are watching football on the couch when I get out of the shower. Each of them has a beer in his hand. I take a seat and join them. We watch most of the game until it's obvious Olympia isn't going to win and Cale gets up.

"All right, I've gotta get up early tomorrow," he says. "I'm going to bed."

"Good night," I say.

After he's gone, Dean says, "Your brother seems cool."

"Yeah. Kind of surprised to see you guys were talking."

He shrugs. "He asked if I wanted a beer and then put the game on."

I nod and watch the commercials for a little while.

"So…what did Myra say about the jump drive?" he asks.

Apparently, bedtime has become our time to talk business.

Chapter Nineteen

"Not much. She seems skeptical, which is understandable, but says she's trying to verify it's real."

He clicks off the TV. "At least she has it. Any idea what else she has on them?"

"No. I don't like having to rely on her for so much." I drop my voice to a whisper. "Besides, she's more focused on finding dirt on Lloyd. She got into politics to help others, and if she sees someone taking advantage of people, she's going to put a stop to it. Bello isn't even on her radar."

"So we'll just have to take care of Bello ourselves."

"Attack his business?"

He nods.

"Human trafficking?"

"We probably couldn't stop that one," Dean admits. "At least, not enough to really hurt him. There are too many people involved and, to be honest, some of the women who are in it don't want to leave."

"Why?"

He shrugs. "It's all they know."

I rub my temples. I can't even wrap my head around it. It makes me sick to think that this goes on in Olympia. And to think it's *normal* for some people.

"I take it Bello's got another business?"

"Drugs, I think."

"What?"

"Word around the street—at least back in my day—is he's a dealer, too. He's not out on the street selling, but he manages a network of dealers. Supplying them with whatever narcotics they need, getting a cut of any profits made in his territory."

"With as much money as he's probably making from the drugs, why does he even still…you know?"

"Business number one?" He shrugs, relaxing his stance. "I don't know. It's the oldest profession, right?"

"Okay, so how can we mess that up for him? Where does he get his supply from?"

"Lots of places, but my guess is it's shipped in something that can be hidden."

FUSE: ORIGIN

"That could be a million places." I think back to the old maps of the city I found with several rail lines snaking through it. Shipping was huge in Olympia, and it still exists today. "How are we going to track down where it's coming in?"

"You got your laptop?"

He follows me to my bedroom. I lay on my stomach on the bed and open my computer.

"Let's look at Google Maps," he says, laying down beside me. "I'm guessing he doesn't want it coming through any other part of the city but his district. So that narrows it down to Hopman."

"Would he be able to unload it in broad daylight without being spotted?"

He shakes his head. "Probably not. It's probably coming in packaging meant for something else."

"Well, that could be anything."

"In Hopman? Not exactly."

I scroll through the few businesses in the district. "Okay, well there's the library, a fire department, a church—"

"Nope, nope, and nope," he says. "What else?"

My eyes grow wide as I follow a railroad spur from the main line right into Wyatt's solar panel manufacturing plant. "It's gotta be Wyatt."

"Why do you say that?"

"The tracks come right into the plant. Easy to hide." I show him the line.

"Damn," he mutters under his breath.

"How—I mean, there are people who work at Wyatt who aren't a part of the family. How is it kept a secret?"

He shrugs. "I don't know. Late shipments? Supervisor inspections? It doesn't matter. What matters is we'll know where the shipment will be, we just need to figure out when."

"And then what? Burn it?"

He shakes his head. "First you break into city hall and then you burn a huge shipment of drugs? Do you *want* to get yourself killed?"

I roll my eyes. One of those was his idea.

"No, it'd just be surveillance," he continues. "You take some pictures, let me know when they're unloading, and I'll give an anonymous tip to the cops to bust them."

"Is there really any such thing as an anonymous tip anymore? They can track your location."

He smiles. "This is where you come in, Mr. Tech Genius."

I guess this is what I signed up for.

"How are we going to find out when this shipment comes?"

His hand rubs against the stubble on his neck and chin. "I may have a few connections. We'll see. I'll need to be careful, though."

"Is there another way that doesn't get you involved?"

He points to the couch. "I'm already involved. I'll be fine."

"Okay. Maybe I can find blueprints of the plant somewhere on Wyatt's servers so I can figure out the best location to hide out."

"Good idea. What about getting inside?" he asks.

I chew on my top lip as I consider. Using my own key card wouldn't work. Even if it let me in, that'd be evidence putting me there. I could use someone else's. Someone who has an alibi already.

"Emma's card."

He raises his eyebrows. "Wait a minute, that's a bad idea."

I shake my head. "No. She's in the hospital. People can vouch for her. Meanwhile, her key card is sitting unattended at home."

"Is it at home? I thought she was coming from the plant when she was attacked?"

"Shit," I mutter. "Um . . . I can stop at the hospital tomorrow and see if I can snag it."

He nods. "Hopefully by then I'll know when the shipment is coming in."

"Yeah."

He rolls off my bed. "Never mind. You're having a hard time focusing your eyes, and I'm beat. Let's go to bed."

My eyes have gotten heavy without me realizing it. The three hours of sleep are showing. I close my laptop and rub my eyes. In the living room, Dean makes his bed on the couch.

I shuffle toward the bathroom but stop in the doorway.

Fuse: Origin

There's something I need to say. Something I'm sure a well-rested Ethan wouldn't say.

"I really appreciate you helping me. I know I'm letting you stay here, but compared to what you're doing for me, it doesn't really compete."

"Don't worry about it." He tosses a pillow on the couch. "It's what friends do."

Chapter Twenty

I've had a chance to review your progress since you returned to work last week," Mr. Duffy says the next morning. "While I'm impressed with the amount you finished in such a short time, I couldn't help but notice you still failed to make up this month's quota."

He paces behind his desk with a copy of my reports in his hand.

"Yeah, I know, but I've been working overtime and weekends trying my hardest to get it all done," I plead.

"I can appreciate that, but at the end of the day, I need to be the one to justify these reports to the board," he says. "They don't want to hear excuses. They want to see numbers."

My chest burns, and I feel like I'm six inches tall in the large leather chair across from his desk.

"I understand."

He shakes his head. "I was told you were a good worker when I started, but I haven't seen that side."

I'm mad, but mostly at myself. I put myself in this situation. I'm the only reason I'm sitting here right now. It's embarrassing,

FUSE: ORIGIN

and I can feel the panic begin to set in. What am I going to do now?

He takes a deep breath and says, "I'm afraid I have to let you go. The rest of the team will have to pick up the slack to make up the month."

All I can do is nod. The lump in my throat tells me my voice isn't reliable. I've never been fired before. Cale is going to kill me.

"Please clear out your desk and stop back up here to sign the termination papers."

With my head low, I silently return to my desk and gather my things. I spent three years here. Met Emma here. This is the only adult job I've ever had. And I'll never come back here.

It feels like I'm in a dream as I walk to the elevator lobby. I can see several eyes watch me as I carry my box through the office. Only a couple weeks ago everyone was welcoming me back. Things have changed so much since then.

———

WITH MY NEWFOUND unemployment status, I'm heading to the hospital to see Emma. The lobby is buzzing with people heading to appointments and waiting for loved ones to finish up their exams. I've been here several times now, so even in my defeated state I can make my way through the labyrinth of hallways that is the First Olympian Medical Center.

Emma is lying alone in her room when I get there. Some of her bandages have been removed, though spots on her skin still look shiny and bruised. The breathing tube is still there, as are the few wires hooked up to various parts of her body.

I remember the nights we'd spent in each other's beds. The sound of her steady breathing as she slept comes back to me. The low murmur of her heart. The signs of a healthy woman.

I force my attention away from her. I need to nab her key card before anyone notices. Locating her few belongings on the table opposite her, I rummage through them.

My mother's words ring in my ear: "You *never* go through a woman's purse!" Sorry, Mom, but this is something I have to do.

Chapter Twenty

Luckily, I'm not searching long before I find it. Slipping it into my back pocket, I turn toward the doorway as Theresa appears.

"Oh good, she fit into your schedule today." She's holding a coffee and stirring in her additions with a tiny red stirrer.

I'm definitely not in the mood for a lecture. "I come as often as I can."

"Really? Because, from what Emma told me, you guys saw each other daily. Now all of a sudden you don't have time for her?"

"It's not like that. I've been . . . working on stuff."

She rolls her eyes.

"But trust me that everything I'm doing is for her."

"It's not me you need to explain yourself to." She points to her sister. "What are you going to tell her when she wakes up? When she asks what happened while she was out? Who was here to visit her? Are you going to tell her you only came by when it was convenient? That even though she went out of her way to see you every day you were in the hospital, you couldn't muster the courage to be there for her?"

Staring at the floor, I've forgotten the reason I came here. It doesn't matter. Theresa's right. I've let Emma down. Even if I do bring down Michael Bello and the Hopman branch of Olympia's mafia, that won't make me a better boyfriend.

I didn't sit by her side every day like she did for me. Instead, I avoided her, feeling sorry for myself. Even now, I can't help but think how bad of a day it is for *me*, as if Emma's having the time of her life in a coma.

Theresa sighs and wraps me in a hug.

"Ethan, we're all scared and worried about her," she says in my ear. "But the best thing we can do for her is be here."

Maybe that would be the best thing for her, but every time I see her, I can't help but see how those men broke her. How even as much as we all pretend it's going to be okay, it's not. She's changed forever. And I don't know how to accept it.

"I see they've taken off some of her bandages," I say when as she steps away. "Is she doing any better?"

Fuse: Origin

She sucks in her bottom lip and looks down at her coffee. "There's a chance that she's never going to wake up."

"What?" My body seems to go numb.

"The doctors say she's unresponsive to a lot of the physical tests they've been running. Reflexes and stuff like that. They told us yesterday that there's a surgery they can do to alleviate some of the swelling in her brain, but it's risky. My parents haven't made a decision yet. It's kind of a losing battle."

I sink down into the chair beside the bed. It doesn't seem like any of this can be happening. Despite my efforts, tears roll down my face. I can feel Theresa's eyes on me, but she doesn't say anything. Neither of us do. The room is silent except for the beeps and whooshes of the machinery keeping Emma alive.

With my newfound free time, I sit with Emma. It might be the last moments I have with her. Besides, I miss her. So much. I may not be able to hold a conversation with her, but being with her and holding her hand helps. For the moment, that's enough.

———

WITH ALEX'S ATTITUDE toward me and my mission, I feel guilty for shoving it in her face by using her lab. But I don't want to risk an explosive fight with Cale by going home, so the clinic is the only option.

I picked up a burner phone on my way from the hospital. Since Dean will likely be making the call from the clinic to tell the police where the delivery is taking place, I need to alter the phone so the location is hidden. I need to make absolutely sure that Alex's clinic won't be identified at all, so I plug the phone in so that I can load the code I wrote to it.

The computer dings, alerting me that the phone is ready to test. I dial my number from the burner and watch my cell phone until the call comes through.

Location unknown.

Simple enough. Now I just need to get rid of the call history from the phone so *I'm* not tracked.

"Still making that death wish?" Alex asks from just behind me.

Chapter Twenty

I jump and drop the phone to the floor with a loud clatter.

"What?" I ask, annoyed.

"What are you doing? Wes said you just showed up without saying hi. This isn't *your* clinic, you know."

"I know. I'm sorry for overstepping, but I needed a quiet place to work."

"What's wrong with the library?"

"I need to make phone calls."

She takes a seat next to me. "What are you even working on?"

I indicate the burner. "I blocked the location from the phone, but now I need to make sure the call history is deleted."

"Why?"

"I called it from my phone to test it."

She picks up the burner and looks at it a moment before setting it down. "Should I even ask what this is for?"

"Um . . . " I hesitate. She's not going to like that I'm still pursuing this. "I found out there's going to be a shipment of drugs coming in to Wyatt's solar plant a few blocks over."

"So why don't you call the police now and tell them?"

"I want to catch them in the act."

She studies me. "Does this have anything to do with the crime family you've been chasing?"

"It's just drugs."

"I don't think it is. Who told you that?"

"Dean."

"And how does he know?"

I shrug. "He just does."

"Look, if you want to run around in some costume pretending to be a superhero, then that's on you. I've said my peace about it. But please don't put me, my patients, and my clinic in the crosshairs."

I shake my head. "You won't be."

"In the time I've been here, I've replaced three windows and lost several pieces of equipment. Ethan, it's hard enough having a clinic in this part of town. I think it's important to keep it open, but don't make it harder for me."

FUSE: ORIGIN

Words escape me. I had no idea that the clinic had been subjected to so much vandalism.

She sighs. "I'm not saying it's all your fault, but you're not helping."

"Alex, I appreciate everything you've done for me, but this is just something I have to do."

"For Emma?"

I nod.

"Really? You're still using her as your excuse?"

"What does that mean?" I thought Alex understood my relationship with Emma. I guess not.

"For someone who claims to be doing everything for this girl, you don't talk about her very often."

"I just don't want to talk about it."

"Really? Do you even realize how bad she is?"

I try not to think of the details. "Yes, as a matter of fact I just saw her this morning."

She snatches the key card from the table. "To steal this? Take a look at yourself. Lying, stealing, getting involved with drug smugglers. This isn't you."

The lump in my throat doesn't seem to swallow.

"Ethan, this is serious."

"So am I!" I shout to the floor, unable to meet her look of disappointment.

"So what's your plan, then? Huh? You're going to go get yourself killed because something bad happened to Emma? That's self-destructive."

Finally, I look up at her. "You don't have to be a part of this."

She studies me a moment. "I want your stuff cleared out of here by the end of the week. If I see you after that, I'm calling the cops and I'm telling them everything."

My breathing is heavy as I watch her head upstairs. There was once a time when I considered Alex my friend. That's not the case anymore.

I feel hopeless. In one day, I got fired and I got yelled at by two different people—and I deserved every bit of it. I can only imagine the hell Cale is going to give me when he finds out about

Chapter Twenty

Wyatt. I have nothing left to do but to press on. If I don't, I'm afraid of the place I'll go.

Dean's name pops up on my phone as it vibrates on the desk. With a deep breath I answer it.

"Tonight," he says. "During second shift."

I nod and then add in a voice that's not quite mine, "Did you find out how it's being kept a secret?"

"Gordon Alistar. He's the supervisor. Most of the men who work second shift are in on it too."

"Oh. Okay. Thanks."

"Are you okay? You sound funny."

I clear my throat. "Yeah, I'm fine."

He pauses, likely not believing me. Then he asks, "Did you find the blueprints?"

"I found a fire exit map. It shows the tracks in the building and the loading docks. It looks like there's a utility bridge that runs the length of the building. I should be able to hide out there."

"Good. Is everything else in order?"

"Uh, yeah. The phone should work fine." With the train coming tonight, I don't have any more time to play with it.

"Okay good. Listen, I think it's important that you get into position early, just in case the train comes early."

The clock in the corner of the ancient desktop reads 5:30. Second shift is in full swing. I need to get moving.

"Okay, I'll suit up. But, uh, we might want to find a different place to operate from," I suggest.

"Why?"

I wipe up some of the dust from the keyboard. If I dive into the story of my day, I'll lose all confidence. It's already barely there.

"Never mind. The com is all set up here anyway. You know how to work it, right? I don't want to lose contact."

"Yeah, I'll be with you the whole time."

———

Fuse: Origin

GETTING INTO POSITION was easy enough. The plant is large and spacious inside, subdivided by several departments and offices. The raw materials are dropped off where the rail line comes in and then immediately go into the assembly line.

I got here about an hour after Dean called, and most of the men are down near the tracks. There are still distant noises of the automatic mechanics moving in another department, but near the tracks below, the men's voices echo throughout the room.

Their conversations don't seem out of the ordinary. They chat about work, families, plans for the weekend. Even though most of them know they're aiding an illegal activity, it's still just another day to them.

From outside, the roar of the train whistles as it crosses Solar Drive, which was aptly named after Wyatt's plant. Another moment later, it slowly rolls into the plant before coming to a complete stop.

Pulling my phone out, I hit record on the video and wait patiently. As part of my tech tinkering at the clinic, I scrambled the identification properties of my own phone so any photo or video I take can't be linked back to me.

The men pull up the ramps, open the cargo doors of the train cars, and begin pulling off the equipment they need to continue to make Olympia an electronic city.

Fifteen minutes pass by before anything suspicious happens. As the men cut into the boxes, they pull out irregularly shaped bags stuffed between the equipment for the solar panels. A couple other men collect the bags and take them into the office. I zoom in and snap a few pictures while still recording. Pointing the camera toward the office, I watch as one man talks on the phone while the other men pile the bags in the corner. I snap more pictures.

"You there?" I whisper into my com. I don't know how much my voice will carry in the cavernous warehouse.

"We're here."

"We?"

"Alex and Wes are here too." Dean sounds annoyed, but I don't push it.

Chapter Twenty

"Make the call."

"You think you can get out of there without being noticed?"

"Yeah, I've got—"

"Hey!"

I nearly drop my phone to the cement floor below. Turning, I see the man approach. He's wearing a gray trucker hat with his safety glasses tucked into the collar of his white uniform.

"What the fuck do you think you're doing up here?" he bellows, drawing the attention of the crew below.

I turn and run as quickly as I can away from him. I came in from his direction, so I have no idea where I'm going. With fire protocols, I'm assuming there's a second entrance. I think I saw one on the map earlier.

Maybe.

Hopefully.

"It's the Halloween man!" he shouts.

Gunshots fire from below. All of the shots miss me and Gray Hat.

I'm sprinting blindly down the catwalk, desperately searching for an exit. There's a door at the end. Maybe it leads to the roof. I hurl myself toward it, but it's locked, and my body slams into the heavy steel. I steal a glance behind me and see Gray Hat is nearly fifteen feet away. Too close.

My palm opens and I let loose a small burst of lightning, busting a hole where the doorknob should be. The surge of electricity leaves me energized, invigorated. But Gray Hat is almost on top of me.

I fling the door open to the roof of the lower level and take off in a sprint through the growing darkness. I know that if I can reach the edge of the roof, I can leap onto the top of the train and find a ladder down to the ground.

The jump to the train is farther than I thought, but I don't realize that until I'm flying through the air, hoping I don't mess up my landing. I may be able to shoot lightning from my hands, but I can still break my leg.

I land hard on my shoulder, smacking my face against the top of the first cargo car on the train. I grip the metal bar running along the edge of the car to keep from falling. At least I'm alive, for whatever that's worth. I look back and see that my pursuer is not as brave as I was. Or as stupid.

More gunshots. The men have moved out of the plant. I slide down the ladder to the pavement on the opposite side of the train. I just need to make it to the fence. That'll buy me some time to lose them. Hopefully by then the police will be here.

Just as I break out into a run, I hear a gun fire from behind me. I glance over my shoulder and see another man in a white uniform on my tail. The suit Wes designed helps me focus my energy to the palm of my hands.

It happens in a split second—turning, letting energy flow through my hand, and the man falling to the ground. Another man who was chasing me stops by his side and I sprint away, gasping for breath but refusing to stop.

Police sirens fill the air and Dean's voice is in my ear, asking if I'm okay and what's going on. I ignore them all and just keep running, hoping I haven't just killed another man.

After I vault over the fence, I take a moment to look back. The sirens are loud, likely on the other side of the train. Under the mask, I smile. I did this. The police will see the drugs and arrest the men. It's the first step in bringing Bello down.

I turn and start running again with newfound energy.

CHAPTER TWENTY-ONE

L ast night I was restless. Tossing and turning, unable to get the image of the man I struck out of my head. Or what I'm going to do without a job. Without Emma.

Cale's gone to work early when Dean and I get back from the gym.

"You can get in the shower first," I say.

"Aren't you going to be late?" he asks.

"No one's expecting me anywhere. I got fired."

His jaw drops. "What? Because you took that week off? I thought you were making up for it."

"Wasn't enough. Look, I don't want to talk about it, really. It just happened."

"Okay," he says with a nod and turns toward the bathroom. Just like that, the topic is off the table.

When he comes out, I add, "I still haven't told anyone else yet."

"How mad is your brother going to be?"

"Pretty pissed. I'll have to look for another job, but I don't think the three years I spent at IT tech support will get me very

179

far. On paper my skills look like I'm just a call center rep." I sigh. "I may have to take Mr. Rizzoli's offer. I'd be doing exactly what I wanted for more than I was making at Wyatt."

He lets out a deep breath, clearly disapproving. "Look into other options first."

"Okay."

"So what are you doing today, then?"

"I don't know. I have to get out of the house, though. Maybe head to the library or something." I don't really know what else to do. And with Michael Bello potentially getting put away, I have no other plans.

Dean sets off for work and I take a shower. By the time I'm done, my phone buzzes with a text from Dean.

Look at the Tribune's *website.*

I pull out my laptop and load the site. The first headline reads, *Major Drug Bust in Hopman* and is dated early this morning. As I read through the article, I smile brightly. Our plan worked. It's as if I can feel the weight lift from my shoulders. Despite everything that went wrong yesterday, I did something right.

The police seized over two thousand pounds of various narcotics and arrested three men at the scene. Tucker Cross is quoted as saying that the bust helps fill in some missing pieces for other drug rings in the city, even identifying some of the biggest drug dealers.

One of the men arrested was apparently treated for third-degree burns—I sigh in relief that he's not dead—from an attack from a man in a black bodysuit. The writer goes on to talk about the other sightings of him—me—throughout the city, most notably my visit to city hall a couple days ago. Surprisingly, the article makes no mention of Wyatt Industries specifically, even though it lists the address. It makes me wonder how much Wyatt paid them to leave their name out of it. Then again, with the Martellis having their fingers in a lot of businesses in the city, possibly even the newspaper, it was probably already an unspoken rule.

Even though I know that the Martellis would try their hardest not to have any of their own incriminated in the papers, I'm still disappointed that there's no mention of Michael Bello. But even if the family wasn't involved, there would be no reason to name Bello. He wasn't at the scene, and until Myra pulls through with the evidence I gathered for her, he's not going to be connected. This mission wasn't to incriminate him. It was to implode a portion of his business before we move on to the next.

I hit reply to Dean's text. *That's awesome! I needed to see that today. No mention of Bello or Wyatt.*

Didn't think there would be, he replies. *At least it's a start.*

True. It's a start. Since I was electrocuted, this is the first positive thing to come out of it.

———

EVEN THOUGH I want nothing more than to meet up with Dean to discuss our next move, I know I need to get to the hospital. It's heartbreaking to see Emma laid up like she is, but it's not about me. It's about being there for her. Like Theresa pointed out, Emma did the same for me.

Theresa's reading in a chair in the corner when I get there.

"Hey."

She lifts her eyebrows, but otherwise looks unthreatening. "Hey."

"How's she doing?" I run my hand along the bedspread.

Shoving a business card in her book, she sets it down on the table beside her and looks at her sister. "Nothing's changed, really."

"Oh."

"Yeah," Theresa says with a sigh.

I suck on my bottom lip and force myself to look at Emma. Really look at her. She's so still and doesn't quite look like herself with her hair down and without her glasses. She's lost the color in her face, and unless the monitor told me that she was alive, I'd think she was a corpse.

I clear my throat to get Theresa's attention. "I want to apologize for not coming as often as I should. You're right, I should be here."

"Ethan, you don't owe me anything. I don't need your

apology. I don't need anything from you. But if you cared for Emma on any level, you'd be around more than you have been."

My voice is thick and small. "I know. It's just—"

"Hard, I know," she interrupts. "But how do you think it feels for me? After work every night I'm here because I love my sister and I'm afraid no one else will be by her side. And my parents? Forget it. They're both inconsolable. And yet they still manage to get here more than you, and they live in Terry Lake, not just a few blocks away."

I nod. My chest is so tight I feel like I want to explode. "You're right. I'll try to come more often. But you've got to believe me when I say that everything I'm doing is for her."

She studies me.

We're quiet for a long time, only the sound of Emma's monitor and the conversations outside the room filling the space between us. If Emma were awake she'd be worrying about something or another. Getting back to work, inconveniencing everybody, whether her plants were getting watered. She'd ramble and giggle and remove any worry we have just by being her awkward, adorable self.

"You know, my father and I don't really get along," Theresa finally says.

"Really?"

"It's not like we hate each other. We just don't really know each other."

"Oh." I don't know where she's going with this, but I let her talk. I imagine it has to be boring to sit alone in a hospital room every night. Her mind has probably gone to a million places and back.

"When I think back to when Emma and I were younger, he's never in any of my memories. It was my mom who took us to the park. It was me and Emma riding our bikes to the corner and back. My dad? I remember him coming home, eating dinner in silence, and disappearing to his bedroom. He'd be snoring within ten minutes."

"That's a shame." Both of my parents were always around. They both worked a lot, but they were there for me and Cale as much as they could be. Up until a few weeks ago, I really had it made. It's a shame I didn't realize it then.

"Yeah. My point is, even to this day, my father thinks he took such good care of us. And he did, to an extent. We never went hungry, we always had a place to call home, and we could indulge every once in a while on vacations or whatever else. He spent his life providing for us, but in the end, all we ever needed was him."

Ah, there it is. And with it, more guilt. But this is different. I'm protecting Emma after a very real attack. She'll never have to worry again once these people are taken care of.

Still, I wonder if part of the reason our relationship will be different after she wakes up isn't because of her injuries, but because of how guilty I feel.

———

"DID YOU HEAR anything at work about the drug bust?" Cale is waiting for me when I get home. He texted me several times today, but I just told him I'd talk to him later. Guess now is later.

I take a seat at the counter and rap my knuckles on the granite.

"What's wrong?" He leans down on the opposite side, trying to meet my eyes.

"Well, I've been meaning to talk to you about that."

"Ethan, just tell me."

"I got fired."

"What?" he shouts and stands up straight. "How could you get fired? Is this because you took that week off without telling anyone?"

"I was making up the work, but I couldn't get to it all—"

"So what do we do now?" He crosses his arms. "You expect me to pay for everything on my own? I'm not a fucking charity."

I fight to keep my composure. I knew he would have this reaction. If we both start yelling, it's only going to push us further apart.

"I have another offer," I say.

"So why haven't you taken it?"

I sigh. "It's not that simple."

"What isn't? Money? That's not simple? You don't have a job, Ethan. Get one, or you're going to have to move back with Mom and Dad." He turns to his bedroom.

"I think the guy who offered it to me is in the mob."

Stopping in his tracks, he turns around and asks, "Why's that?"

"It's just a hunch. But look, you're going to get promoted soon and you'll be making a lot more money."

He returns to the kitchen and takes the seat next to me at the counter. "I don't know that I am. The Works story is drying up, and I need something if I'm going to get that anchor position."

"Myra still won't help you, huh?"

"No. We really got into it a few days ago, right after that weirdo in the suit broke into city hall. She doesn't want to mix her professional and personal lives. She won't admit it, but I think that guy in the mask scared her. I would be! She thinks I'll be in trouble by knowing her."

I can relate to that.

"I feel like she just doesn't want to be exposed as the source," he continues.

"Can you blame her?"

"But if she tells me, she knows I wouldn't do that!"

"Cale, think of it from her side. Being a city councilman's assistant is not her dream job. Anyone who talks to her for more than five minutes knows she has bigger plans. If she starts disregarding her principles with you, who's to say she won't do the same with someone else? And just like that she becomes another politician like everyone else."

He rolls his eyes. With the Works story, I'm sure he's run into a lot of the political runaround.

"Besides," I add, "you might not be the one to expose her, but someone will likely discover your connection. Your job as a reporter might not be compromised, but hers as a public figure probably will be."

Sighing, he says, "I guess so." We're quiet a moment and then

Chapter Twenty-One

he asks, "So you're unemployed now?"

I stare at the countertop. "Yeah."

"And that job offer is no good?"

Shrugging, I say, "I don't know. I still have to think about it some."

He rubs his face and then puts his arm around me. "I guess we'll just have to work it out."

I smile. "Thanks, Cale."

"All right," he says as he gets to his feet, "I've gotta go find something that'll save me from getting fired."

"Why don't you give Tucker a call? He was quoted in the *Tribune*."

"He was?"

"Don't you read the news? It was front page."

He snatches up his phone from the counter and looks through his contacts. "I'll give him a call."

"Why don't you go down to the station yourself?" I suggest. "He's your friend. Take him out to dinner or something."

"I don't want to date him, I just want the scoop. Stuff I can put on camera."

"Then take your camera!"

"You're right." He checks his watch. "He should still be there, right?"

"Unless they had a bigger break in the drug case, I think he's going to be working longer hours."

"Great, I'll see you later. Thanks, Ethan!"

It's good to know my brother still has my back, even if he is disappointed I lost my job. But then, Cale has always been there for me.

There's a knock at the door and then I hear, "Ethan, it's Dean."

Scooting off the barstool, I let him in.

"You know, maybe I should just find a new place to live," he says. "I feel like this arrangement is inconvenient for everyone. I could hire a moving company to clear out my old place so I'm not spotted."

"Don't worry about that just yet. You're fine." I don't want him to go. On my walk back from the hospital I realized that

Fuse: Origin

Dean's been a tremendous help since everything happened with Emma. Not only with distracting me from the consuming sadness—which was nearly unbearable yesterday—but also with helping to give me purpose. Something to fight for. I don't want that to end.

Besides, if Dean really is being watched, it'd be safer for him if he wasn't alone. At least, it would make me feel better. After what happened to Emma, I don't want to lose anyone else in my life.

"Are you sure?" He eyes me warily.

"Yes, don't worry about it."

"Okay," he says as he exhales. "We need to move quickly with Bello."

"What do you mean?"

"His drug business is in a state of shock. The boss will want him to lay low, but Bello is too headstrong. He'll want to regroup, send some men after your alter ego and rub him out."

"Yeah, but how does that help us?"

Dean rocks his head back and forth. "He's probably meeting with the men under his jurisdiction."

"Okay, so let's say he is meeting with all of his subordinates. The question is, where and when?"

"Soon. Bello works a regular job. He needs to keep up appearances. But he'll want to meet quickly. It'll likely be tonight."

I'm surprised and my palms begin to sweat. Going after random people who don't expect me is one thing, but it's another to actively seek out a meeting designed to plan your murder. Not to mention, I'm tired. I don't want to run from gunshots tonight. But that's my role now that I have this ability. The news that the man didn't die last night is empowering.

"Okay, but where?" I ask.

"A small family establishment in Little Italy. That's my guess, anyway. It was Bello's favorite place when I knew him, and he's a creature of habit."

I roll my eyes. "Of course."

He flashes a quick smile before saying, "Bello's going to be skittish, so he's going to have lots of men protecting him."

Chapter Twenty-One

"Do you think I can take them?"

"Definitely not."

Just like that, my empowerment is crushed. "Thanks for the vote of confidence."

"That's why I'll be there to back you up."

"What if they recognize you?"

"They can't talk if they're dead," he says with a smirk that terrifies me.

"I don't want people to die."

The smirk fades. "That came out wrong. It's just—these men are not good people. I'm not going there for a bloodbath, but I'm not going to hesitate to shoot one of these fuckers down if it comes to it."

I nod wordlessly.

"See if Alex and Wes are willing to help out," he says, shifting gears. "We could use an extra set of eyes watching security cameras."

"I really don't think they'll help." Wes isn't really my concern, but Alex made her views clear yesterday. Besides, I'm not even sure the grid reaches up to that point in the city yet. The solar roadways are still being installed down the major corridors.

"She's just worried about you, man," he says, reading my thoughts. "That's all."

"I guess you're right. I'll give her a call." I escape in my room and hit send on her contact information on my phone. It rings twice before she picks up.

"Ethan, hi." She sounds odd. Hesitant almost.

"Hey, I know you made things clear yester—"

"Forget about that." She cuts me off. "Do you have a minute to come down here and talk? It's...uh...kinda urgent."

"Uh, sure. I might have a little time."

"Cool, I'll see you soon."

When the line goes dead, I look at my phone for a moment before returning to the main room with Dean.

"She wants me to go down and talk to her."

"Why?" he asks.

"I don't know. But she said it was urgent."

Fuse: Origin

"Okay, but we've gotta move quickly. Bello's likely called a dinner meeting, so we don't have much time. Meet back here in an hour and we'll go from here. Sound good?"

I nod, still nervous. "Yup."

He grabs my arm. "Hey. We've got this."

———

SURPRISINGLY, THE LIGHTS are already off at the clinic. Sometimes Alex closes down early if there's no one there, but there usually is.

The door's unlocked and I let myself in the back. The sound of voices leads me to the reception desk. Alex is leaning against it with her arms folded, talking to Tucker.

"Ethan!" Alex calls when she spots me. "I'm glad you could come so fast."

Tossing a thumb over my shoulder, I say, "I don't have a lot of time. I was actually hoping to talk to you in private for a few minutes."

Tucker turns to me and offers a tight smile. "Ethan."

Alex looks between us. "Um, there's actually something you should know first."

My heart races again. I shove my hands in my pockets to keep them still, but I can tell it's not hiding anything. What more can be thrown my way?

Alex must've found something in my blood work. Something that didn't manifest right away. Or maybe something happened with Emma. Or Cale. Or Myra. Suddenly I feel like I need to sit down, but I lock my knees and try to act casual.

Tucker clears his throat. "Dr. Fletcher tells me you've been hanging out with your physical therapist."

Well, that's a twist. My eyes narrow and I look between the two of them. "What's going on?"

Alex rubs her hands together. "Dean knows a lot about . . . the Martellis."

Oh dear God, Tucker knows my secret. How could Alex betray me like this? I trusted her. I didn't think our blowout

Chapter Twenty-One

yesterday was enough for her to go right to the police.

"I knew you were . . . curious about them and were asking around." She's choosing her words carefully. "It seemed like once you met Dean, you started acting differently. I got suspicious."

"Alex, what did you do?" My voice is low, almost a growl.

She chokes up and Tucker continues for her.

"She was worried about you, Ethan. After the two attacks against you, both related to that family, she wanted to make sure you weren't making things worse for yourself."

I run my hands through my hair, unable to keep them still. I want to leave, to run, but there's nowhere to go. Mostly, I want to make sure that Dean's okay. That there isn't a police crew waiting for him to turn the wrong corner and arrest him.

But what would he be arrested for? I'm afraid to admit it to myself.

"Someone needs to tell me what's going on," I finally say.

Tucker hands me a photocopy of a police report from several years ago. A younger Dean stares at the camera with a mugshot. "Dino Martelli" is listed right above his charge: grand larceny.

"No, this has to be wrong. His last name is Adams."

Tucker looks at me with sympathetic eyes. "Adams was his mother's maiden name. But Dean's father is Carlo Martelli."

CHAPTER TWENTY-TWO

I lean on the back of the couch and chew on the inside of my lip as I watch the door and wait for Dean to arrive home. A mix of emotions run through me. Betrayal, denial, anger. It just makes too much sense for it not to be true. How could I be so stupid?

Before I left the clinic, I put the suit on under my clothes. I had planned on taking Dean's bike to the restaurant, but that's different now. I don't know how I'll get there. Taxi maybe? The subway will be too crowded this time of night.

What if this whole thing tonight is a trap? What if Dean is purposefully leading me there to suffer the same fate as Emma?

As much as I tell myself to give him the benefit of the doubt, I can't. Why I didn't I see it before? I didn't want to see it. You don't find out that much about a crime family's dealings by simply joining for a little while. And even if you did, there's no way they'd let you out with that kind of knowledge.

Luckily, the suit is doing its job and keeping the electric charges surging through my body at bay.

The knocking at the front door tells me that Dean's back.

Chapter Twenty-Two

Reluctantly, I let him in, even if all I want to do is lock him out.

"Hey," he flashes a smile. "What'd they say?"

"Fuck you." Not the best opening line, but it pretty much sums it all up.

His eyebrows scrunch together. "What's the matter?"

"How long did you think you'd be able to keep it up, huh? Do you think I'm just that stupid that I wouldn't figure out who you really are?" Apparently, I was that stupid. God, I hate myself right now.

The color drains from his face. "How did you—"

"It doesn't fucking matter how I found out! It's true, isn't it? You're a Martelli? You're fucking one of them!" I'm shouting now, the full extent of my anger shining through.

"You didn't tell the cops, did you?"

I want to hit him. Punch him right in the face. Again and again until everything goes away.

But it won't fix anything. He's still a liar.

"I gave you a place to stay, I helped keep you safe from the men in your family who were coming after you!" I shake my head. "I stuck up for you."

He follows me farther into the apartment, and the thought of hitting him crosses my mind again.

"Ethan, wait! I meant to tell you! I wanted to. You're just not—"

I spin on my heels and get into his face. "I'm not what? Not smart enough? Not strong enough?"

What's surprising is he's not angry. He looks sad. Probably even scared. He should be. But tonight there are more important things to think about. That is, if I'm not walking right into a trap.

"Get out." My chest heaves.

"What about tonight?"

"Just stay the hell away from me. You're not the person I thought you were."

He hesitates a moment longer and then leaves.

———

Fuse: Origin

"YOU'RE STILL GOING?" Alex's annoyance with me is likely through the roof right now. But I can't just sit home. Especially now. I need to let out my anger, and what better way to do that than to take it out on the man who thinks he owns the city and its women?

"I have to," I mutter into the phone. My taxi passes between glass-faced skyscrapers that open up to the twentieth-century-style Broadway district, also known as Olympia's Little Italy.

"Did you listen to a word we said today?"

"I'm going alone."

"Oh, well *that* makes me feel better!"

"This never had anything to do with Dean. It was always Emma."

"And I'm sure she'll love having you as a roommate down-town!"

"This is just something I have to do. I need you to watch the cameras for me and let me know if anything happens while I'm there."

"You're an idiot, Ethan."

Ain't that the truth.

"Are you going to help me or not?" My voice is small. I don't know what to think anymore. My world has completely changed. Going through with the mission is the only thing that'll keep me sane. I have to keep pushing on.

"I'm going to call the police. Maybe then we'll get through that thick head of yours."

Sighing, I say, "You do what you need to do."

I hang up and think of my new backup plan if she *does* call the police. I'll just have to scope it out more before I head inside. Listen for the sound of sirens coming in my direction. We pull up to the address I told the cab driver. I hand him the money and get out.

The building across the street from the Little Italy Food Company holds a nightclub. Being that it's Tuesday, the place is empty, which allows me to stealthily climb up to the roof and strip off my street clothes so I'm just in the black suit.

I pull out my phone and scope out the neighborhood via

Chapter Twenty-Two

Google Maps. Not the best way to gain intel, but it's all I have.

Luck is on my side, and the sun has set so my dark clothing hides my location on the opposite rooftop. I check the time. Just after seven. It's later than the original plan was, but it might work out in my favor.

By the looks of it, most of Bello's soldiers are inside already. As long as the capo himself doesn't leave first, I should be set to nail him. I just wish I knew how many bodyguards there are and what kind of heat they're packing.

From my vantage point, I can't quite make out what they're doing inside, but I see people start to stir, so I assume the meal is over.

It's now or never.

Taking extra precautions, I hop along the roofs of two nearby buildings until I can't see any of the hidden bodyguards that might be in the area. Then I climb down a fire escape and sprint across the street. I cut through the small alley behind the row of buildings until I'm in the loading area behind the restaurant.

"Hey!" The man at the back door calls to me after I jump the fence and land on the pavement. He points his gun at me. We're only five feet apart. The closest I've ever been to the opposite end of a gun. Even the man I killed stood farther away from me.

With newfound confidence, I step toward him and throw my palm against his belly. A trickle of electricity flows through my fingers and he convulses for a minute before collapsing silently to the ground. I kneel beside him and make sure he's still breathing.

After dragging him around the corner, out of sight, I hold his gun in my hand and consider keeping it. It might do me well inside, but since I don't intend to kill anyone, I toss it in the dumpster and head inside.

The lone waitress freezes when she sees me. I put a finger to where the mask covers my mouth.

Now what? I can't just tell her to be quiet and hope she listens.

That's when I spot the cook too. His face doesn't show fear, yet he doesn't approach me.

Fuse: Origin

"What do you want?" he asks.

I allow a trickle of electricity to zap between my fingers. Nodding toward the freezer, I wave them both inside and shut the door behind them. Man, I feel like a jerk for that, but I need them out of the way. I can't let them get hurt too.

The plexiglass window in the kitchen door allows me to see right into the dining room where several men are embracing and others are shaking hands.

It looks like a reunion or a birthday party. Smiles and well-wishes. You'd never know what these men are capable of. They each leave one by one, with Bello remaining to talk to a man whose face I haven't yet seen.

That's when I feel the cord slip around my neck and tighten, pulling me to the ground. I grasp at the cord, but it's too tight. Through my blurry vision, I see a big man with dark skin lean over me and slam his fist into my face.

Chapter Twenty-Three

My face is on fire as the remaining men in the dining room each take a swing at me. Blood and saliva drip from my swollen lip, and I can't see out of my left eye. My stomach is queasy from the taste of blood. I think I've swallowed a tooth.

"Oh, look at that, Superman's awake," one of them says.

"Look at the poor bastard. Didn't expect this, did ya, kid?" They laugh as another one hits me again.

I'm a toy to them. Nothing more than something they can play around with and then toss in the trash when they're done. Just the way they treated Emma. I hate them all.

"All right, let the kid breathe." From what I can tell, he's the only man here without any blood on his hands. None other than Caporegime Michael Bello. "He's got questions to answer."

"What the hell are you doing here, kid?" an older man asks. He was the last one to take a swing at me before Bello stopped him, and he's wiping my blood off his hands with a cloth napkin.

Summoning all of my courage, I scowl at him as best I can. Which results in a roar of laughter from the room.

Bello smiles. "You know, we've heard stories about the man in the suit. Fuse, as people have been calling you. But what we just couldn't figure out was what the hell you wanted."

He circles the room as the four other men stand threateningly around me.

I need to think. How the hell am I going to get out of here? I can't contact Alex—if she's even there—because my mask is lying on the floor at one of the men's feet.

"It's funny, too," Bello continues, "because if you would've told me back at Rizzo's dinner party that the scrawny kid asking about the newest shiny building in the city was Fuse, I would've laughed in your face. In fact, that's just what I did when Sammy took off your mask." He addresses the men, "Isn't that right?"

I hate him. I hate him. I hate him.

He kneels down in front of me. "So tell me, what made you want to put on some tights and prance around my neighborhood after dark?"

"You hurt a friend of mine." I must've bitten my tongue because my words come out thick.

Bello smiles. "Ah, I see. Lover's revenge." He steps back and studies me. "Wait a minute, you're talking about that Landry girl, aren't you?"

If I could shoot electricity through my eyes, I would right now. He knew her name, and yet he still isn't losing any sleep for putting an innocent woman in the hospital.

"You broke her," I finally say.

Shrugging, the capo says, "Well, her injuries were a little more permanent than what I thought would happen, but they still did the trick. And we thought your meeting with the boss straightened you out. But it turns out you were just playing dress-up!"

The men laugh again, and I struggle to break free of the zip ties holding me to the chair.

"You had no right to touch her!"

"Oh, you really are clueless, aren't you? We run this city. There isn't a thing that goes on around here that we don't know about. Including your friend."

I narrow my eyes. "What does that mean?"

He smirks as he pulls out his cell phone. "We control her fate."

Chapter Twenty-Three

"What are you doing? Who are you calling?"

Bello holds up his finger to me. "Clip her," he says into the phone. He scrunches up his face. "I'll straighten it out with him, just do what you're told."

Everyone looks dismayed, and I try to tell myself that he didn't just say what I think he said.

"I had a doctor friend of mine personally take on your friend Emma's case." He holds the phone out to my ear. "Why don't you check in on how she's doing?"

No. This can't be happening. She's not—

Sammy puts a finger to his lips and I fight tears.

It's quiet, and then a monitor shrieks in the background. I hear Theresa call for a doctor.

"Oh my God, Emma!" she cries.

"Ma'am, please step back," someone else says.

"Heart rate's dropping," another says.

I turn my head, but Bello pushes the phone against my ear as I listen to the doctors struggling to revive her. I know what's coming. And there's nothing I can do to stop it.

When the long beep of the monitor indicates Emma's heart has stopped beating, Bello pulls the phone away from me.

"I told you. We control everything."

My body shakes with remorse, anger, sadness, and a million other emotions. My chest aches, and the taunts from the room seem like distant voices as the world slows.

Just like that, Emma is gone. Forever erased from this world. To the man who called for her death, her life didn't matter.

Like waking from a dream, the jeers and laughter grow louder. I shoot my power out of the palms of my hands, striking the floor as I try to pull away from my restraints.

It's no use. The most I'm doing is scuffing the floor. Yet I catch everyone's attention.

"Oh, and Fuse goes wild!" Bello grabs my face tightly in his hand. "I could use you to power my next building—since you seem to be so interested in where this city is going."

Glass shatters and my chair tips to its side. Bello cowers until he disappears out of my sight.

FUSE: ORIGIN

I keep my head low to the ground as gunshots fill the room, sending shards of glass across the floor of the restaurant. I hear two thumps behind me. Only one man is in my line of vision. The fourth must've run with Bello.

With the sound of gunshots only a ring in my ears, I look up and see Dean hovering over me. He slips a knife between my wrists, cutting the zip ties and finally freeing me.

"How did you—"

He hands me my mask and offers his hand. "Come on, we're not done."

Slipping it back on, I hear Alex's voice in my ear. " . . . please answer me."

"I'm here," I say as I get to my feet. I sway a little.

"You okay?" Dean asks, pushing at the swinging door to the kitchen and peeking inside. I notice a handful of zip ties tucked in his back pocket.

I force myself to press on despite the throbbing in my head. This is it. The moment I've been working toward. I can't let Bello slip through my fingers.

"I'll be fine," I say and follow Dean through the kitchen and out the back door.

"Are you okay?" Alex asks. "What's going on?"

"Not now."

I vault over the fence behind the restaurant, trailing Dean. Bello and his bodyguard are farther up the alley in the back of the buildings. I extend my arm out, sending shockwaves toward Bello and his bodyguard. Success.

Dean sprints to the guard and restrains him while I dive onto Bello, screaming at him with each punch.

"You're! A! Fucking! Murderer!"

"Hey, take it easy," Dean warns as he struggles to keep the guard still.

We hear men's voices coming from the restaurant, and Dean, who has finally managed to tie up the guard, pulls me back behind a dumpster. There's fifty feet between us and the street entrance.

The gunshots start again. Dean shields himself and fires back at them, keeping them at bay. I lean back against the dumpster, my head pounding worse than ever between the noise and the running. Meanwhile, Bello is curled up in himself as he crawls to his own safety.

"I already called the police," Alex says.

Pressing the com against my ear, I say, "What if we don't get away from here in time?"

"I thought you were dead!" she yells in my ear.

Dean turns back beside me, his chest heaving.

"Alex called the cops," I tell him. "We need to keep these guys busy until they get here."

"What's our exit plan?" he asks, casting another look around the dumpster.

I point to the alleyway. "I think it's our best shot."

He eyes it for a moment and then nods. "Okay. I don't know how much ammo I have left, so you might have to take over. You good with that?"

Before I answer, the gunshots stop. The sirens seem to be almost on top of us now. Time to move.

"Let's go," I mutter to Dean. Peeking my head over the dumpster, I see that the four men are almost on top of us. As they raise their guns to fire, I send bolts of lightning their way. They all duck long enough for us to sprint down the alleyway and around the corner. Shots fire onto the street, but they don't follow us. A police car pulls up moments after we run out of there.

Dean's bike isn't far, which I'm thankful for. I'm lightheaded from all the running, but I focus on getting to the hospital.

———

THE SIGHT OF Emma's family sobbing immediately brings me to tears. But it's my swollen face that draws their attention.

"Ethan, what happened?" Theresa asks.

I shake my head and let the tears flow. Theresa wraps an arm around me and the four of us cry, dumbfounded.

"I don't get it," she says. "I was sitting right there! Everything was fine. The doctor said she was doing well and then . . . "

"I should've been here," I say. I know I couldn't have been

by her side when it happened, but I still wish I had been. At the very least, for Theresa's sake. I can't imagine how terrifying that must've been.

"Ethan, don't," Mr. Landry says. "We all wish—things should've been different."

Even as I begin to mourn Emma with her family, it doesn't quite seem real. As morbid as it sounds, I haven't even seen her body. The hospital staff moved the Landrys down to a private bereavement room where time seems to stand still.

I lose myself in my sadness, forgetting how I ache or the hell I went through earlier this evening. None of it matters anymore. This was all for her, and she's the one I lost in the end. If I hadn't gone after Bello, she would still be alive. Knowing I provoked this tragedy is a brand new kind of hell.

Mrs. Landry's gentle hand cradles my face. "We should get this checked out."

"I will," I tell her.

We linger for a long time, none of us really ready to leave and face the world, yet all of us knowing that we should. Theresa offers to have us all over at her place, but I pass.

I know they lost a daughter and a sister, but none of them had the chance to save her. I did. I tried. And I messed it up. Their pain is on me. I can't grieve with them and pretend like I'm one of them. I can barely look the Landry's in the eyes knowing I'm partly to blame for their suffering.

As I walk through the lobby, Frank Lloyd's picture on the TV catches my eye.

"City councilman Frank Lloyd has been removed from Olympia City Council after evidence indicates he had dealings with a prominent crime family," the news reporter states.

The city's mayor, Eugene Banks, is shown at a press conference. "We were presented with a thorough file of everything he's done in the last four years that's been questionable, and it all lines up with instances involving organized crime."

The reporter returns. "The investigation is now in the hands of the Olympia Police Department, however Mayor Banks says Lloyd's removal from the council is necessary with the amount of evidence against him. Lloyd's term would have expired with the next election. No word yet on who will fill in as his replacement."

I turn to leave, but the next story stops me. Michael Bello's bruised face is displayed on the screen. His mugshot.

"The man behind some of the city's biggest success stories as of late, including the Lakeside Village condos and the redevelopment of Ashland Pier, has been arrested for suspicion of murder. City police detective Tucker Cross and his crew responded to a 911 report of shooters at the Little Italy Food Company in Broadway's Little Italy tonight. Police at the scene say there are at least three dead. No further details are known at this time."

That smug bastard. He finally got what was coming for him.

———

THE APARTMENT IS silent. My phone is still in my bag on the roof across from the restaurant. The place is probably crawling with police officers and reporters by now. If they find it, I'll be brought in, questioned, maybe even arrested myself. Hopefully they found the cook and the waitress in the freezer.

The ride from the hospital back home seems to take forever. I'm fighting back tears with everything I have. I'm not about to cry in front of the cab driver. He's already watching me with a wary eye because of my face. I stumble through the front door and—

There's movement in the shadows to my right and my heart races. It's someone from the Martelli family. They must know I was the one there tonight. They're pissed. I'm dead.

He moves from the shadows and the light catches his face enough to reveal it's Dean. I'm not even mad at him right now. I'm just relieved I'm not going to meet Emma's fate. I keep trying to convince myself that she's really gone, but I just can't quite grasp it.

"I got your bag," he says. "A lot of people have been calling you."

I wipe my nose, suddenly self-conscious. Dean never knew Emma. How can I expect him to be sad about it?

"How are you?"

FUSE: ORIGIN

All I can manage is a shrug.

He stands there awkwardly, my bag still in his hand. "I can leave if you want. I just thought it was probably best if you weren't alone. But maybe you should call your brother or—"

"It's fine," I say in a thick voice. "You can stay."

He nods and takes a seat beside me. "I'm sorry for not being honest with you right from the start. I should have told you a million different times. I wanted to, but I—"

"It's fine." I wipe my eyes with my sleeve, taking extra care around my left eye.

"It's not. But believe me when I say that that's *not* who I am. I might've been born a Martelli, but I'm not a part of the family. Everything I told you about them breaks *omertà*."

It's the last thing I want to think about right now. At this moment, I'm just glad he's here. If Cale or Myra were here, they'd be cooing and telling me that everything will be all right and Emma's in a better place. Dean just lets me grieve.

We sit quietly for a long while. My phone buzzes a few times. Calls from my family, Emma's family, our friends. I can hardly think right now, let alone talk to anyone.

"How?" Dean finally asks, breaking the silence.

My eyes remain locked on the hardwood. "Bello called someone at the hospital, gave the word, and had her killed. He had me listen to the whole thing."

"Oh, Ethan." He pulls me into an awkward hug and I lean into it, wrapping my arms around him tightly as the tears start to flow again.

"She would've been fine," I croak by his ear.

He rubs my back and squeezes me. "You did everything you could."

"I messed it up."

Pulling me away from him, he holds my face in his hands. Our eyes meet and my heart beats a little faster. It all seems so surreal—Emma's death, my role in it, this moment.

Which is why I don't react when I feel him place his lips on mine.

———

Behind the Book:
FUSE: ORIGIN

I often get inspired by TV shows. The visual aspect of it really helps me spin off ideas in my head when I start to commit a story to paper. *Charmed* inspired the Under the Moon series. *Nashville* inspired *A Christmas Reunion*. *Arrow* inspired this book.

Growing up, I was never into comic books. I knew the basic stories of Superman, Batman, Spider-Man, and the rest, but the comics themselves didn't interest me. My brother and I used to watch all the animated superhero shows before we got on the bus in the morning, but that was it. (Years later, when I actually read the iconic comics like *Batman: Year One*, I realized that the cartoons were not that far off from the original comics. So I guess I had my taste back then.)

I knew that if I was going to write a superhero book, I needed to do it right. That's why I did some research by reading the comics, watching the TV shows and movies, and really trying to determine what happened in each medium to produce an awesome product.

Fuse: Origin

A couple things I discovered:

- The title character always had an origin story, even if it was revealed later.
- The superhero always had an impossible mission to fulfill (Batman's mission to rid the city of Gotham of corruption, Spider-Man's mission to clean up the streets of NYC).
- There was always something tragic tied to the mission.

Another important aspect was that these stories took place in an urban environment. Often fictional (at least in the DC Comics universe), these cities played an important role in the superhero's world. Plus, in a fictional world, you can really make your own rules to challenge your characters.

Since I love looking at maps, I set out to make my own fictional city. Using several different poster boards taped together, I spread it across my dining room table and got to work. It made me think of the different aspects that make up a city. Its culture, history, pitfalls, successes. What started as a couple pencil lines on paper developed into a full-fledged city.

I wasn't sure if I wanted to completely dive into the world of super powers. Another show that inspired this series was *The Flash*, but I found I didn't enjoy it as much as other superhero shows because it seemed *everyone* had super powers. What makes the superhero so special if everyone has powers like that?

So I created a different kind of villain. Drawing from the Batman comics, I created an organized crime family. This took even more research into how crime families work: how they make money, how they avoid arrest, what sort of pressure is felt by each person of the family.

It was a lot of fun (and work!) putting all of these pieces together. Actually, the first six chapters were written without an outline, way back when I was writing the first draft of *The Full Moon* in the fall of 2014. I set *Fuse: Origin* aside (then called *The Shocker*) to work on the Under the Moon series and then picked it back up two years later in the fall of 2016. This time, though, I outlined the rest of the book, which took on a completely different direction than where I thought it was going.

Fuse: Origin was a fun book to write. It's a whole new set of characters to play with. A fresh slate. And, as you can probably guess from the title, it's just the beginning.

———

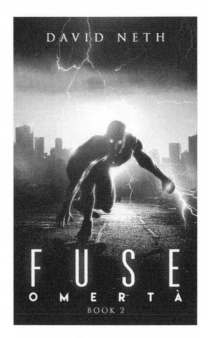

Still reeling from the shocking murder of his girlfriend, Fuse managed to put Michael Bello behind bars. But only days later, the murderer strikes a plea deal and is out. Now, he's disappeared from public view. Ethan vows that justice will be done and starts the pursuit once again.

But another fiend is stalking the streets of the city; someone who leaves his victims stripped of their very skin. So far there are two victims and Ethan fears that the next will be someone he cares about. And the clock is ticking.

———

Available in ebook, paperback, and audio!
DavidNethBooks.com/Omerta

MORE BY THE AUTHOR

To find the rest of the author's books visit
DavidNethBooks.com/Books

———

Subscribe to his newsletter to be the first to know of new
releases and special deals!
DavidNethBooks.com/Newsletter

———

If you enjoyed the book, please consider leaving a review on
Goodreads or the retailer you bought it from. Reviews help
potential readers determine whether they'll enjoy a book, so
any comments on what you thought of the story would be very
helpful!

ABOUT THE AUTHOR

David Neth is the author of the Fuse series, the Under the Moon series, and other stories. He lives in Batavia, NY, where he dreams of a successful publishing career and opening his own bookstore.

———

Follow the author at

www.DavidNethBooks.com
www.facebook.com/DavidNethBooks
www.twitter.com/DavidNethBooks
www.instagram.com/dneth13

Made in the USA
Columbia, SC
19 March 2018